"What

"You!" Molly exclaim

Clay made a mock bow.

But it wasn't the flesh Molly remembered. She hated to see he'd turned out good-looking. He should have been fat and bald as punishment for the crimes of his youth.

He drew her onto the dance floor.

"Relax, Molly. For tonight, let's pretend we're old friends."

She'd never been in Clay's arms before, and a realization suddenly dawned. Part of her problem was that she was wildly attracted to him. She tried to control her feelings or turn them off. She failed.

"You're holding me too close, Cusak."

"We've never agreed on anything, have we?" Clay said with an intimate laugh. "I was just thinking it wasn't close enough."

Dear Reader,

It's time to celebrate! This month we are thrilled to present our 1000th Silhouette Romance novel—*Regan's Pride*, written by one of your most beloved authors, Diana Palmer. This poignant love story is also the latest addition to her ever-popular LONG TALL TEXANS.

But that's just the start of CELEBRATION 1000! Throughout April, May, June and July we'll be bringing you wonderful romances by authors you've loved for years— Debbie Macomber, Tracy Sinclair and Annette Broadrick. And so many of your new favorites—Suzanne Carey, Laurie Paige, Marie Ferrarella and Elizabeth August.

This month, look for *Marry Me Again* by Suzanne Carey, an intriguing tale of marriage to an irresistible stranger.

The FABULOUS FATHERS continue with *A Father's Promise* by Helen R. Myers. Left to care all alone for his infant son, Big John Paladin sets out to win back the woman he once wronged.

Each month of our celebration we'll also present an author who is brand-new to Silhouette Romance. In April, Sandra Steffen debuts with an enchanting story, *Child of Her Dreams*.

Be sure to look for *The Bachelor Cure*, a delightful love story from the popular Pepper Adams. And don't miss the madcap romantic reunion in *Romancing Cody* by Rena McKay.

We've planned CELEBRATION 1000! for you, our wonderful readers. So, stake out your favorite easy chair and put a Do Not Disturb sign on the door. And get ready to fall in love all over again with Silhouette Romance.

Happy reading!

Anne Canadeo
Senior Editor
Silhouette Romance

Please address questions and book requests to:
Reader Service
U.S.: P.O. Box 1325, Buffalo, NY 14269
Canadian: P.O. Box 1050, Niagara Falls, Ont. L2E 7G7

THE BACHELOR CURE
Pepper Adams

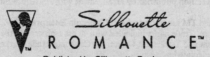

Silhouette
ROMANCE™
Published by Silhouette Books
America's Publisher of Contemporary Romance

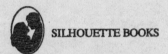

SILHOUETTE BOOKS

ISBN 0-373-19003-4

THE BACHELOR CURE

PEPPER ADAMS

lives in Oklahoma with her husband and children. Her interest in romance writing began with obsessive reading and was followed by writing courses, where she learned the craft. She longs for the discipline of the "rigid schedule" all the how-to books exhort writers to maintain, but does not seriously believe she will achieve one in this lifetime. She finds she works best if she remembers to take her writing—and not herself—seriously.

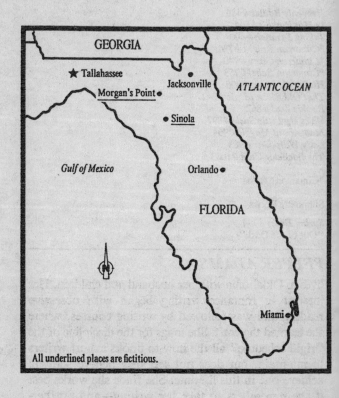

All underlined places are fictitious.

Chapter One

The cork popped out of the champagne bottle with a half-hearted little whoosh. Clay Cusak shook his head wryly; that underwhelming display of pizzazz would undoubtedly set the tone for the rest of the evening. A bottle of bubbly had seemed like a good idea when he'd ordered it from room service an hour ago, but he'd since lost his enthusiasm for celebrating.

The mirrored wall of his hotel suite reflected his frown, and he noticed the network of tiny lines fanning from the corners of his eyes. That's what came of spending too many hours in the Florida sun.

And of being thirty years old. Today.

The lines weren't so noticeable when he smiled, and that made him feel better. He eyed his reflection critically. At least his hair hadn't started going gray. Or had it? No, it was still dark blond; those lighter strands were due to sun-bleaching, not advancing age.

He set the wine bottle down and made an exaggerated show of flexing his muscles to reassure himself. They were firm and well defined. Not bad for a guy who spent five and a half days a week in a pharmacy counting pills. Of course, the remaining day and a half usually involved sailing or other water sports.

He turned his back to the mirror. What was his problem? He never brooded or felt sorry for himself—he wasn't the self-absorbed type. Maybe it was the occasion. He'd heard people often turned introspective on their thirtieth birthdays.

Thirty! That wouldn't seem old to some people, but it gave Clay pause. Adulthood had taken him by surprise, and now that he was officially in the midst of it, he feared something might be missing from his life.

He wasn't sure what. All in all, things were going well. He was on the road to financial stability and it was leading him away from Morgan's Point. Lately he'd felt there was more to the world than the small town could offer. As he'd approached thirty, he'd become itchy, ready for a change.

For five years, he'd been content to run the drugstore he'd purchased shortly after graduating from pharmacy school. Now he wondered if he might have settled down too soon. Maybe he'd played it too safe, never taking the risks that could have added excitement to his life.

Originally he'd bought the pharmacy because it was for sale and he was a pharmacist. He'd inherited some money and he liked the idea of being his own boss.

The fact that it was located in his mother's and friends' adopted town was a bonus.

An astute businessman, Clay had expanded the menu of the soda fountain, enlarged the inventory and stocked a line of home medical supplies. When profits had exceeded expectations, he developed a five-year financial plan. His investments were conservative at first, mostly secure small-yield venues. Then he'd met a great-looking redhead who happened to be an investment counselor. She'd shared her expertise, and he'd learned a lot.

So far, he'd been lucky. Only one year had passed and he was already ahead of schedule. He just had to keep himself focused. Sometimes he got so caught up in the melodrama of his customers' lives he forgot how unsatisfying his own was. But there were always moments like this to remind him.

"Cheers!" He clinked his glass against the empty one on the tray. Restaurant and hotel personnel couldn't think in numbers less than two. One for dinner was frowned upon, but one for champagne was almost ignored.

He should be used to it by now. Although he went out often, he chose not to share his little celebrations with the women he dated. Why give them a sense of permanency in his life when he had no intention of asking them to share it?

He was happy with the way things were. He liked doing what he wanted, when he wanted. His ultimate ambition was to become a crusty old bachelor, bumming around in the Keys and fishing all day. That is, if you would call living on a yacht "bumming."

It was all part of the plan. If he lived simply and invested most of his income, it would work. Unless the bottom totally dropped out of the investment market, he could retire in style while he was still young enough to enjoy it.

He wouldn't be like his father, who had worked hard all his life, never taking time to enjoy his family or anything else. All in anticipation of retirement at age sixty-five, after forty years of service to the same company. Only then would he have time to do what he really wanted. But life had played a dirty trick on Walter Cusak; he'd died at sixty-four, three months short of that magical day. His widow now lived comfortably on his accrued pension.

Recalling the futility of his father's life made Clay even more determined to make his plan work. He took another sip of wine. He wasn't a workaholic, nor even overly ambitious. But he was conscientious, and he enjoyed the freedom that money made possible. He'd decided a long time ago that it was better to do things than it was to accumulate things.

His carefree ways had endeared him to many. Hadn't someone once said that friends were the reward of a long life? Clay liked everyone and everyone liked him.

When he leaned back on the settee, his mirror image mocked him, one eyebrow raised skeptically.

"Okay, maybe not everyone," he amended. "So there's no love lost between me and Molly Fox." He grinned. That was a nice euphemism for the long love-hate relationship he'd shared with his childhood friend's older sister.

Clay topped off the glass again and offered a wry toast to his absent nemesis. "Here's to you, Molly. The only female who didn't succumb to my irresistible wit and charm."

He took a sip of wine, recalling with pleasure why he'd come to Miami. Oh, there was the pharmaceutical conference and an important lecture in the morning he didn't want to miss. But the real reason for the trip was a chance to look at a sixty-foot yacht. According to the good-old-boy grapevine, the owner needed to sell and it was a steal. Even though it would be a while before he could afford it, it never hurt to look.

A look was all he had time for. He had to catch a plane to Jacksonville and hurry back to Morgan's Point. He'd promised his friend Rachel that he'd be home in time for her sister's reception. Normally he loved parties, but this one he could do without.

He anticipated meeting Molly, now a physician, with both dread and expectancy. He hadn't seen her since his high-school graduation; she'd gone off to medical school shortly afterward. She'd always been an unresolved element in his life, mainly because she had never paid him the attention he thought was his due. No matter what he'd done to capture her interest, she'd ignored him. She hadn't laughed at his practical jokes. In fact, she'd treated him even more callously than someone as obnoxious as he had been deserved. He could only hope that her taste in men had improved over the years.

The hate part of their love-hate relationship had been mostly on her side, and Clay had never reconciled her lack of warmth. He prided himself on amiability, but his good nature had often been tried by Molly's unreasonable rejections. Since she was four years older than him and Rachel, he'd assuaged his budding adolescent ego by ascribing her contempt to her self-important teenage hauteur. Well, they weren't teenagers anymore.

Clay opened his briefcase and pulled out the leather-bound notebook where he recorded his personal financial information. In it, he'd plotted his schemes and devised the plan by which he could leave the workaday world behind and go sailing off into the sunset. Alone. He rechecked the figures and was satisfied with his calculations. His good humor was fully restored. He had a plan and nothing could stop him now.

Not even Molly Fox's imminent and much celebrated arrival.

The bright overhead lights had been replaced with chinese lanterns. Bunting decorated the walls, and butcher paper covered the long tables. A mouth-watering array of homemade dishes filled the buffet table. The focal point of the high-school cafeteria was a handmade banner spanning one wall. It read, "Welcome Dr. Molly!" in big blue letters.

Molly Fox was touched that the citizens of Morgan's Point had gone to such lengths to greet her. She was also a little sorry that she couldn't seriously consider their request to stay and establish a family practice in the newly constructed clinic. She should have told them that right away, but everyone had been so gracious she hadn't had the heart. When the town council upped the ante, making the offer even more attractive, she promised them she would consider it.

As the party progressed, Molly began to suspect that her arrival wasn't the only reason for the celebration. Obviously the people of Morgan's Point were glad for the chance to congregate and have fun. In a town this size, they had to make the most of every social gathering.

During the course of the evening, Molly was introduced to so many men, women and children that she finally gave up trying to remember names and faces. It seemed that every person in town made a point of paying their respects to Lydia's daughter and Rachel's older sister. She was happy, and a little envious, to know that her family had found such a pleasant place to call home.

"Are you feeling guilty yet?" Rachel asked from across the table where they'd gathered to eat.

"No," Molly replied with a grin. "Was that the reason for this little shindig?"

Her mother, Lydia, laughed nervously and changed the subject. "I'm so happy the three of us are together again. It's been four long years. Isn't it a lovely party?"

"It certainly is." Molly turned to her sister. "I know you went to a lot of trouble, Rachel, and I appreciate it. It couldn't have been easy to do while suffering from morning sickness."

"I couldn't have done it without Joe." Rachel smiled at her husband.

Joe Morgan, mayor of Morgan's Point, wrapped his arm around Rachel's shoulders and pulled her close to his side. "The Ladies Auxiliary did most of the work, and Clay Cusak raised the money for the decorations and such.''

Rachel squeezed her husband's hand. "Where is that rascal? He promised he'd be here.''

"Don't get upset on my account," Molly said. She'd been a little surprised to learn that Clay had been involved in the preparations. Such a magnanimous gesture didn't sound like the Clay she remembered. A frog in the punch bowl was more his style. "Clay was never one of my favorite people.''

"Molly!" Lydia exclaimed. "What a perfectly awful thing to say. Clay is a wonderful boy and he's always been a good friend to this family. Hasn't he, Ernie?" she asked in an effort to bring her new husband into the conversation.

Ernie only nodded; he was a man of few words.

"'Boy' is the operative word," Molly said. "Like Peter Pan, Clay Cusak will probably never grow up. I'm surprised he's made it to the ripe old age of thirty. I should have done him in myself for all the nasty little tricks he used to pull on me.''

Rachel laughed. "Remember when you were thirteen and he put those bath-oil beads in the back pockets of your jeans?''

The memory made Molly grimace. "When I sat down at school the beads burst and it looked like I'd wet my pants. It was a heartless thing to do to a teenage girl.''

"Especially one as preoccupied with her image as you were," Rachel added.

Joe, always the arbitrator, said, "That was a long time ago, Molly. Clay was only nine then. Surely you don't still hold his childish pranks against him.''

"Oh, yes, she does," Rachel said. "I love him like a brother, but Molly always considered him the evil twin."

Lydia sniffed. "Evil? That boy? Why, he had the face of a cherub. And my, how he could talk."

"I'll say," Rachel put in. "He charmed his way out most of the tight spots he got us into and left me, his less eloquent partner in crime, to take the rap."

Lydia shook her head. She'd never taken Clay's pranks seriously. "He was just a lonely little boy clamoring for attention."

Molly knew her mother had always had a soft spot in her heart for Clay, an original latchkey kid. She'd been like a second mother to him when the families had lived next door to each other in Jacksonville. Somehow he had replaced the son she'd lost as an infant.

"Is he still?" Molly asked. "Clamoring for attention, I mean?"

Rachel laughed. "Most of the time."

Molly turned to her brother-in-law. "You'd better watch out, Joe. Clay used to propose to Rachel on a regular basis, starting in third grade. Now that you two are married, he must be plotting to get rid of you."

Joe shook his head. "I'm not worried. Clay and I understand each other."

Before Molly could question him further, a commotion in the front of the room drew their attention. Some of the men were shoving back tables and others had rolled in a piano.

Rachel leaned forward. "Those are the Dudley twins, famous for their dueling fiddles. Miss Watkins, the home-ec teacher, plays piano. Surprisingly enough, they're pretty good."

The trio proved it by playing some lively tunes that soon had a few brave souls on the dance floor. Small children tapped their toes and wiggled their behinds to the beat. It was a charming gathering, and Molly wasn't immune to the warmth and fellowship that filled the room. It occurred to her that she had been given the opportunity to become a part of all this, but she wasn't sure she would fit in as easily as her mother and sister had.

The lights dimmed, and the music slowed to a waltz. Rachel and Joe excused themselves to take a more active role in the socializing.

Ernie nudged Lydia and asked, "Want to dance, honey?"

Lydia started to stand up, then realized that Molly would be left alone and sat back down again. "Not just now."

"Go on, Mother, I don't mind. I'll just sit here and enjoy the music," Molly insisted. She kept a careful physician's eye on her mother as the older woman walked out to the spot that had been cleared for dancing. She seemed as steady on her feet as she'd ever been. It had been a year since she'd been involved in an auto-pedestrian accident. Lydia claimed she had fully recovered, and it appeared that she had.

As Molly hummed along to the old familiar tune, a strong hand gripped her elbow and pulled her from her seat. "What's up, Doc?" The deep masculine voice was filled with amusement.

"Stop," she protested, swinging around to give the offender a piece of her mind. "Oh, it's you."

Clay Cusak made a mock bow. The grin was the same, the face more mature and hardly cherubic. "In the flesh."

But it wasn't quite the same flesh Molly remembered. Clay had always been her biggest aggravation, and she hated to see that he'd turned out so darned good-looking. He should have been fat and bald as divine punishment for the crimes of his youth.

"I don't care to dance just now," Molly said firmly.

Clay clucked reprovingly. "Still chilly after all these years?" He leaned close and she caught the scent of his woodsy cologne. "You know, people are beginning to stare. If you sit down now, they'll be honor-bound to gossip about us."

Molly knew he was right; she could feel the interest around her. She worked herself up to a halfhearted smile. "Why, yes, thank you for asking, Clay. I'd love to dance."

Clay had been pleasantly surprised when he'd first seen Molly Fox across the room. The Molly he remembered had always had her nose stuck in a book, when she wasn't tattling on him and Rachel for some imagined grievance. Those beautiful gray-green eyes should have been distorted behind thick lenses from reading too much.

Instead, they shone with vitality and intelligence. Her dark lustrous hair fell loosely to shoulders bared by a peasant-style blouse. Her lips, which he'd often imagined pinched from perpetual disapproval, were full and sensuous. She was as beautiful as ever, perhaps even more so now that the years had lent a mature grace to her classic features.

It was hard to believe that this was the same old Molly, his childhood nemesis, despoiler of good times. But it was. And she could still make him feel like the awkward teenager he'd been the last time he'd seen her.

"I hope you're satisfied, Cusak," she said as he waltzed her flamboyantly onto the dance floor. "Everybody's watching us."

"Good." He grinned down at her. "It's gratifying to know you can still freeze the extremities off an Eskimo with your icy glare. Can you anesthetize patients with that look, Doc?"

"No, but it's been known to stop trains and clocks, as well as discourage assorted assailants."

"That's what I figured." His eyes were filled with the mischief she remembered from their childhood. He'd always looked like that right before she found a garter snake in her book bag or a page missing from her secret diary. She wished she felt half as detached as she sounded.

Time had touched Clay, but gently. As he took her into his arms, Molly tried to recall her last image of him, standing proudly in his cap and gown at his and Rachel's graduation. He was a man now, and tiny shivers of excitement touched her as he settled his body into hers. She tried reminding herself that this was just ornery Clay Cusak, neighborhood pest and bane of her tortured youth, but she wasn't very convincing and the shivers didn't abate.

"Don't look so worried, Molly. I promise I don't have any frogs in my pocket tonight." Clay's breath stirred her hair and he caught the scent of wildflowers.

Molly adjusted the distance between them. This strong virile man was very different from the lanky boy she remembered. He looked different. He felt different. He even smelled different.

He tightened his arms a bit and spoke softly. "Relax, Molly. Just for tonight, let's forget our past problems and pretend we're old friends."

Considering the amazing effect his nearness was having on her, it would be only too easy to forget the past. The darkened room, the dreamy music, the whispers, all wafted around her to block out memories of everything but the moment.

Molly recognized the danger in that and wished Clay wasn't holding her quite so close. She wished that she couldn't feel the heat of his skin beneath her hands and that his lips near her hair didn't give her goose bumps. He was aware of the effect he had on her, and it seemed to please him. His pleasure only annoyed her.

She had never been in Clay's arms before and a realization, distasteful as it was, suddenly dawned on her. Part of her problem stemmed from the fact that she was wildly attracted to him. Her body responded to him in ways it had never responded to any man before. She tried to control her feelings, to turn them off, or at least temper them with good sense. She failed.

She drew back and looked him in the eye. "You're holding me too close, Cusak."

"We've never agreed on anything, have we?" he said with a laugh. "I was just thinking I wasn't holding you close enough."

Before she could react to that statement, auto mechanic Dell Harley tapped Clay on the shoulder. "Mind if I cut in?"

At first, Molly thought Clay was going to object, even hoped he would. Then the musical trio picked up the pace with a fast song, and he shrugged and backed off. Molly took Dell's hand and was whirled away. She watched as Clay danced with just about every other woman in the room. She took a turn with Officer Hacker and several others as the evening slowly wound down and the guests began to drift off.

When the impromptu band announced the last song, Dell Harley was about to claim Molly for another dance, but Clay shook his head and pulled her into his arms. The music was slow and languid, and their bodies moved together much too naturally. His hand slid down her back, molding her ever closer, and it irritated her when her traitorous heart began to pound erratically.

Molly didn't know why Clay wreaked such havoc on her nervous system, but it was clear that he did. And he enjoyed every minute of it.

His hand was hot and suggestive on her back and seemed to burn right through the cotton fabric of her blouse. His lean legs pressed against hers as he rubbed his cheek against her temple. She tried to tell herself that none of it meant a thing to Clay or to her. He was an incurable flirt and she had been alone too long.

A bit shaky by the end of the song, Molly pulled her hand from Clay's and noticed Rachel and Joe waving to her from the doorway as they left.

"Thanks for the dances, Clay," she said as she backed away.

"My pleasure."

She turned around and said over her shoulder, "Looks like my ride is ready to leave."

She started back to the table and he followed her. Molly, anxious to get away from his unsettling presence, picked up her purse and hitched the slim strap over her shoulder. She made an excuse for her abrupt departure, lest he think he unnerved her—which he did. "I hate to keep Rachel and Joe waiting."

"You're not." He took her arm and walked along beside her.

"I'm not what?" she asked, her footsteps quickening as they stepped out into the balmy April night.

"You can slow down—they're not waiting." He gestured at the nearly deserted parking lot. "Rachel was feeling queasy, so I told them I'd take you home."

Molly stopped in her tracks and took a deep angry breath. "Why?"

Clay shrugged. "Too much of Mrs. Pringle's cheesecake would be my guess. She ate three pieces. Joe said she's been craving sweets. A couple of weeks ago, they came pounding on my door in the middle of the night. Made me open the drugstore because Rachel couldn't go back to sleep without having a cherry phosphate."

"Clay," Molly said, exasperated, "why did you volunteer to take me home?"

"Still the same old blood-'n'-guts, cut-to-the-chase Molly, huh?"

"And you still don't have a serious bone in your body, do you?" she parried. "Why did you offer to take me home?"

He'd almost forgotten how much fun he'd had trading quips with Molly in the old days. Some things didn't change. "I've never danced with a woman who made my knees tremble before and—"

Molly laughed nervously, interrupting him. "Still the same old comedian, aren't you?"

He was serious, but he could tell Molly wanted to believe it was all a joke. He knew from experience that it would be a waste of time to argue the point. But he wouldn't lie to placate her. Let her believe what she would.

"I wanted to take you home because it's been twelve years since we've seen each other and I thought we could catch up," he said sincerely. "And because I feel a strange attraction to you." The admission sounded corny, so he wiggled his eyebrows at her and added suggestively, "I was hoping to have my wicked way with you."

"Okay, okay." She held up her hands in surrender. Since beginning her medical training, she had focused her energy on her career at the expense of personal matters. She had managed to avoid involvement over the years by giving men an impression of cool aloofness, a facade that was strangely at odds with the warmth and caring she demonstrated to patients and their families.

She was sensing danger where there probably was none. The problem was that Molly had neglected her physical needs too long and her biological clock was fast becoming a ticking time bomb.

Okay, so what if she was momentarily attracted to Clay, someone she'd disliked in the past? It didn't mean anything. She didn't need to try to frighten away a man four years her junior. She had wiped his runny nose when he was just the brat next door and her sister's little playmate. He was not a threat to anything more than her composure.

When they reached his car, Molly smiled at him. "Okay, so you're just doing a friend a favor. Forget I made such a big deal of it. I'll go along peacefully."

"Don't give in too easily," he teased with a grin. "It takes all the fun out of it."

Chapter Two

Clay's vehicle was a sleek blue minivan with CU-SAK'S PHARMACY painted on the side windows. He maneuvered it expertly onto the quiet street before he spoke.

"So, how do you like Morgan's Point?"

"It seems nice. The people have all been very gracious. They shouldn't have gone to so much trouble arranging that reception."

"We were trying to impress you with our hospitality," he said with a glance in her direction. "Did it work?"

She nodded.

"So, will you be staying on with us, Doc?"

"I don't know yet," she answered honestly. "Morgan's Point is a charming little town. The people are friendly. My family's here . . ."

"But?" he prompted.

"But I'm not sure where I want to settle down."

"We need a doctor, Molly. I guess Rachel and Joe explained how we got the clinic built?"

"Yes, they did." She'd heard it all. Her sister and brother-in-law had worked hard to secure government financing through a rural medical program. But if they didn't obtain a firm commitment from a doctor soon, the federal funds would be withdrawn. According to Rachel, if that happened, the local bank, which had provided interim financing, faced economic ruin. Old Doc Cooley had planned to come out of retirement to help them out, but he'd recently died quietly in his sleep and she was their only prospect.

"I don't want to put any pressure on you," Clay said with an uncharacteristically serious expression. "But to state it simply, a lot hinges on your agreeing to stay. Everything from community health to the town's economic security."

Molly laughed wryly. "Thanks for not pressuring me." She added in a quiet voice, "I'm still considering the town council's offer."

"I'm glad to hear that."

"And I'm glad we've had this chance to talk, Clay. I confess I was a little reluctant to see you again."

"Why?" He wondered if she'd felt the same mixture of anticipation and dread that he had at the prospect of renewing their acquaintance after so many years.

"I never quite knew how to deal with you. You always set me on edge and left me unbalanced. You were quite annoying in that respect, as I recall. You were an awful pest."

Clay turned to her. "Was I really that bad?"

She pretended to think it over. "Only Dennis the Menace could have topped some of your youthful escapades."

"Not true!" he protested.

"I should know," she reminded him. "I was usually on the receiving end of your pranks."

Clay frowned. "Tear one lousy page out of a girl's secret diary and she never lets you forget it."

"And you were responsible for most of the battles between me and Rachel. You were always able to con her into going along with your wild schemes. She's the one who showed you where I hid my diary."

"Guilty as charged. But there were extenuating circumstances. I was eleven years old and caught in the throes of prepubescent turmoil. It didn't help matters that I had a terrible secret crush on you."

"You did not." She looked at him and was struck all over again by how handsome he was. With age, his cute boy-next-door looks had settled into a substantial virility. But his blue eyes still sparked with the mischief she remembered. Eyes that were openly appraising her.

"Yes, I did," he said stubbornly.

"At eleven?" She was skeptical. "You were into magic tricks and toilet jokes."

"Since you paid me all the attention you would accord an insect, I had to do whatever I could to get you to notice me."

Molly didn't have a comeback to that one and wondered if he was still teasing her. By the time he pulled into her mother's driveway, she was embarrassed at having made such a fuss over a five-minute drive. She decided to make amends.

"The lights are still on. Mom and Ernie must have waited up. Want to come in for a cup of coffee?"

"Sure. I wonder if Lydia has any homemade cookies?" he asked as they walked up the front steps.

Molly nodded. "She made some yesterday. When Rachel reminded her you were out of town, she just went on baking, anyway. Hasn't she always baked cookies for your birthday?"

"You remembered my birthday?" he asked. "I'm thrilled."

"I'm not. Just like in the old days, I got stuck washing the cookie sheets when she finished."

Molly opened the door and was surprised to find the living room empty. "I'm sorry, they must have gone to bed and left the light on for me."

Clay looked disappointed. "Does that mean I don't get any cookies?"

Molly smiled, kicked off her sandals and tossed her purse on the sofa. "Come on, Cusak," she said, leading the way into the kitchen. "I'll even make the coffee."

"I like milk with cookies," Clay said, opening the cupboard for a glass. "How about you?"

"I'd rather have coffee, but I'll settle for milk." Molly took the lid off the cookie jar and Clay handed her a plate.

She arranged the cookies on it. "I've been here three days and I can never find anything. You got it right on the first try."

Clay shrugged. "I helped Lydia out after the accident. My mother complains that I spend more time here than I do at her house." He slid open the patio door. "Want to go out on the deck so we don't disturb Lydia and Ernie?"

Molly stepped outside. "Look, Clay, there's something I want to get straight. I would have come home if I'd known Mom was badly injured. She said her leg was broken and when I asked Rachel, she confirmed it."

"That was the truth."

"It was a lot worse than that, and you know it. She suffered some brain damage and had a lengthy rehabilitation. I could have helped if I'd known. I still feel guilty that I wasn't here for her." She sat down on the glider.

Clay sat down beside her and handed her a glass of milk from the tray. "By the time we finally reached you by telephone, Lydia had regained consciousness. She was adamant about not telling you how serious her injuries really were. She didn't want to take you away from your patients. She thought they needed you more than she did."

"I'd hoped to be home by Christmas to see Rachel and Mom get married. But my replacement was delayed and I couldn't leave until last week."

"Everyone understands, Molly. There's nothing to apologize for. Especially to me."

"Mom was always good at getting what she wanted where you and Rachel were concerned."

"Yes," Clay agreed. "And this time what she wanted was for you to be spared the stress of worrying about her."

"So you and Rachel made a decision you had no business making."

"It was Lydia's decision," he reminded her. "Actually, Rachel and I felt you got off too easily. Like the time you poured a pan of dishwater on us for sneaking cookies and we were the ones who had to mop the kitchen floor."

"I may have dripped a little water on you—"

"Dripped? It was a bean pot full of soapy water."

"It wasn't. I'm older and I remember it clearly."

The fact that she'd brought up the difference in their ages made Clay suspect it bothered her. "Your memory seems to be a bit impaired. But I hear that comes with old age. You've conveniently forgotten every despicable thing you ever did, haven't you?"

"What did I ever do to you? Name one thing," she challenged.

"Let's just change the subject."

"Because you can't think of one?"

"Maybe." Clay laughed and offered her a cookie. "Have one of these, Molly. Maybe it will sweeten your disposition."

She caught the teasing glint in his eye as she accepted the cookie. He continued watching her, waiting for her to make a comment, but she didn't have one. Clay had always had a way of tying her nerves up in knots, and it seemed that his technique had improved with age. But now, instead of provoking her to anger, he aroused an equally helpless feeling: unwelcome desire. When she'd been younger, she had dismissed him as an annoying kid. She couldn't do that anymore. Clay Cusak was no kid.

He sighed with mock resignation and stretched his arm along the back of the glider. "For a minute there, I thought we were going to be friends. I'd hoped you'd forgive my past transgressions, maybe even learn to like me a little."

She fought against the smile tugging at her lips. When he looked like that, it was hard to remember that she'd once considered him as desirable as chicken pox. "That's what you get for thinking, Cusak."

He leaned closer until his face was near hers. "Don't you like me a little?"

"Maybe a miniscule, microscopic little bit," she said softly as she pretended interest in her cookie. In an effort to guide the conversation away from her feelings, which she didn't fully understand, she asked, "How's your mother?"

Clay ran a hand through his hair. "Retired with a capital *R*."

Molly cocked her head to one side. "Meaning?"

"She's bored, I guess. She's always worked and now she has nothing to do. Seems to think having a pack of grandkids would be the answer to her dilemma."

"I can't imagine your mother wanting grandchildren," Molly said before she thought. "I'm sorry, I didn't mean that in an ugly way."

"No problem." He grinned. "I was the kid who waited around at the ball field because she got busy and forgot to pick me up after practice."

Molly remembered that day. "When my mother reminded her, Norma was so upset she backed out of the driveway like she was in the Indianapolis 500."

"She wasn't upset. That's just how she drives. She's even worse now." Clay laughed. "If you value your life, don't ever get in a car with Norma Cusak behind the wheel."

"Thanks, I'll remember that." Molly took a sip of milk. "I guess you're elected to provide the grandchildren."

"Being her only child kind of puts me on the spot. For the last two years, she's been trying to marry me off to her friends' nieces and daughters."

Molly imagined that Clay would appeal to a wide assortment of females. "What? Can't she find any takers? Maybe she should offer a cash bonus as an incentive."

"I'll tell her you suggested it. But then, you'll become a potential candidate."

"I'm too old for you."

"It won't matter—you're still single," he said. He put his thumb on her bottom lip and touched it gently.

Molly was filled with renewed awareness of the man sitting so close to her. He leaned forward and his knee brushed hers. She thought he was going to kiss her, and didn't know what she would do if he did. She needn't have worried.

"And I see that you still have all your own teeth. I wasn't so lucky last time," he said seriously.

Molly giggled, something she never did. Obviously her reaction was a result of a release of tension. "You're exaggerating."

"Nope. Mothers are real picky for the first year or so, but when those 'I gotta be a grandma' hormones kick in, anything in a skirt will do."

"You're nuts."

He shook his head. "Wait until you've been in Morgan's Point for a while and Lydia starts in on you."

"I may not stay, Clay."

"I assume you have your reasons."

"I don't want to be the only doctor in town again. The last four years taught me that."

She'd spent those years working for the National Health Service on an Indian reservation in Montana. It had taken her that long to repay the government for financing her medical training. For four years she'd been the only doctor in a seventy-five-mile radius, on call almost constantly. Day after day, she'd dealt with problems that should have overwhelmed her, but somehow hadn't. It had been a rewarding but emotionally exhausting experience.

"To be honest with you, Clay, I don't know if I'm up to waging another solitary battle against pain. I want to work in a modern well-appointed city hospital with the support of highly trained colleagues. It's very trying to always have your judgment on the line. To be responsible for so many lives."

Clay recognized the note of weary frustration in her voice. He'd felt it himself. Owning a business in a small town, like being the doctor, entailed a type of service and commitment that were not required in conventional jobs. It was widely believed that professional satisfaction was an acceptable substitute for emotional fulfillment. His own customers thought nothing of calling him on his day off because they'd run out of medication. Always being on call had definite drawbacks.

Obviously the past four years had been hard on Molly, and Clay knew her fears were legitimate. When he felt trapped, thinking of his plan and the freedom it promised made it a little easier.

"You wouldn't be isolated here," he pointed out. "Morgan's Point is thirty minutes from Jacksonville, not on the back side of the moon."

"I guess I just don't know how I want to spend the rest of my life," she admitted.

"That's your problem," he said.

"Astute observations were always your strong point, weren't they?" she asked drolly.

He shrugged. "Far be it from me to give you career advice. But it seems to me that you already know how you want to spend your life—you're a dedicated physician. Your immediate problem is deciding where. When you're making your decision, just remember the only person you have to make happy is you."

"Are you advocating selfishness?" she asked with mock incredulity.

"Works for me."

"That from a man who gets up in the middle of the night to satisfy the cravings of pregnant women?"

"Satisfying women, pregnant or otherwise, is its own reward," he replied dryly.

Molly sighed reproachfully. "Just when I thought we were about to have a deep meaningful conversation, you make a joke."

"Hey, it's kept me out of trouble for years."

"You'd better be careful," she warned. "Or I might start thinking you're shallow."

"No, women usually have to get to know me much better before they figure out how shallow I am."

He protested too much, making Molly wonder if his banter was just his way of avoiding any kind of emotional involvement. He couldn't possibly be as irresponsible as he wanted her to believe. If he was, he never would have earned the respect and admiration of the people of Morgan's Point.

Molly pressed the issue. "You were such a wild little kid, I never thought you'd go into a profession as serious as pharmacy. I imagined you'd become something less staid. Like a lion tamer or a bungee-jumping instructor."

He grinned. "Actually, I've always thought I'd make a great beach bum. Sailing around the Keys, lazing about, doing nothing but fishing and sipping spiced rum all day."

She eyed him speculatively. "How boring."

"Well," he said defensively, "not everyone is as driven by ambition as the Fox sisters."

"What a tacky thing to say."

"Tacky, but true. And I'll admit that I would hate being poor. That's why I have a plan. So I can have a substantial income without working."

Molly laughed. That sounded more like the Clay she remembered. "Nice work if you can get it," she said.

"And you can get it if you try," he finished.

He was still close, so close that his breath felt warm on her face. So close that Molly could feel his body heat. She knew she should move away from him, find an excuse to say good-night. But she couldn't. She could scarcely breathe.

Clay must have been aware of her reaction, for he pulled away, but not before she saw the confusion in his eyes.

Molly changed the subject to cover her discomfort. "What do you think about Rachel's new husband?"

"Joe's been good for her. I know it sounds corny, but those two were made for each other."

"That's what I thought as soon as I saw them together. You used to propose to Rachel at least once a year. I hope you aren't hanging around waiting for something to go wrong so you can conveniently step in and pick up the pieces."

Clay chuckled. "I'm grateful she had the good sense to refuse me. We dearly love each other and we'll always be friends, but we were never *in* love. Joe and Rachel asked me to be their baby's godfather."

"I didn't know that." She was amazed at how relieved she felt that he wasn't secretly carrying a torch for her sister. She didn't understand why she should be glad. But she was.

Clay stretched out his long legs, putting the glider in motion. "The moon is really bright tonight," he remarked.

"Yes, it is."

He turned his head and gazed at her intently. "Do you like to sail?"

"I haven't been sailing since college," she admitted.

"Then it's time you tried it again. I've got a small boat on Lake Sampson. Let's go for a moonlight sail."

Molly glanced at him to see if he was serious. "At this hour?"

"Why not? The water's calm, the moon's full. It could be very... relaxing."

Molly wasn't sure she wanted to get that relaxed with Clay at this point. "I don't think so."

Clay frowned. "Where's your sense of adventure? Your spontaneity? Don't think about it. Just do it."

"I like to plan these things. Going out on a boat half-cocked at this time of night doesn't seem too smart."

"But it could be fun. And you did consider it, didn't you? For a moment?" he asked as he pulled her to her feet.

It was true. For a moment she had actually considered doing something totally reckless. "You're a bad influence on me, Clay."

She looked up at him, feeling awkward and ill at ease because she knew he was going to kiss her this time. Her heart thudded in her chest and her brain warned her to move away. She disobeyed the warning.

Clay's lips brushed hers lightly, soft and warm, undemanding. When she didn't object, they returned, pressing against her mouth, hotter and more urgent. He pulled her body against his and Molly's skin tingled, strangely sensitive and alive. His mouth moved insistently, opening her lips to his gently exploring tongue. Instinctively her arms crept around his neck and she clung to him, her body melting into his.

He moved his hands up and down her back, and warm pleasure washed over her like a wave, setting her adrift in an unfamiliar sea of passion. No man's kiss had ever affected her quite that way. She was intensely aware of the heat of Clay's body as it moved against hers, of his hard muscles beneath her hands, of his special scent.

Then his lips left hers to trace a path to her ear where he nibbled at her lobe while his hand moved up to caress her breast. For a moment they were alone in the world.

Then Molly heard the sound of her mother's voice from somewhere in the house and remembered where she was. She opened her eyes, and the reality of who she was kissing with such wild abandon came crashing down on her. She removed her arms from around his neck.

"We shouldn't have done that," she said, stepping back. She nervously smoothed her hair and noticed that Clay's face was flushed, that his chest rose and fell rapidly.

Clay took a long slow look at the woman in front of him. Her silky hair was mussed from his fondling, her eyes wide with anticipation and surprise. Her sensual lips, moist from his mouth, begged him to kiss her again, but he didn't.

"I'm kind of glad we did." His voice was husky.

Molly glanced away, she couldn't look at Clay. He probably understood her response to him better than she did, and that gave him power over her. "Maybe you should go, Clay."

He tipped her chin up with one finger and planted a damp kiss on her forehead. "I want to stay."

"No, just go," she pleaded.

"I'll leave," he said as he stepped off the deck, "but I'm not going away." His words surprised him. He was annoyed with himself for making what was dangerously close to a promise. He'd have to be careful. A woman like Molly could pose a real threat to his well-laid plans. To say nothing of his future bachelor status.

Molly followed him around the house and watched as he swung into the driver's seat of the van. He closed the door and lowered the window. As he backed out of the drive, she heard him singing an old song praising the medicinal value of good lovin'. So "good, good lovin'" would cure what was ailing him, huh?

She should feel indignant, but all she could do was smile at the murdered lyrics. Clay Cusak was a very attractive man. His engaging sense of humor and robust appreciation of the weirder things in life were a large part of his appeal. But she would be certifiable if she allowed him to get under her skin.

She returned to the glider and was startled when her mother spoke behind her. "Is Clay gone?"

She pretended to look around, even under the seat cushion. "Must be."

"Don't be fresh, dear," Lydia said, shifting her pet duck in her arms as she sat down next to her daughter. "Why didn't you go sailing with him?"

"Mother! Were you listening to every word?"

"At my age? I was lucky to hear half of the conversation from that distance." She gestured at her open bedroom window.

"Maybe you should get a hearing aid," Molly suggested with a grin. "What's wrong with Mrs. Puddleduck?"

"Nothing. Ernie let her inside for a few minutes and we were just about to put her out, but then you and Clay drove up, so we slipped back into the bedroom. We didn't want to spoil the mood, you know?"

Molly reached out to stroke her mother's pet, but drew her hand back when the duck flapped its wings. "I wondered why she didn't come out of her house. I assumed she was being her usual antisocial self."

"Puddleduck isn't antisocial. She just doesn't know you yet. Now stop trying to change the subject and answer my question. Why didn't you go sailing with Clay?"

Molly shrugged. "It didn't seem like a good idea."

"Too romantic for you?" her mother suggested.

"Give me a chance to get used to the idea. Clay Cusak was a thorn in my side the whole time we were growing up. I spent years trying to avoid him. It's hard to voluntarily choose his company."

"Clay's a very nice young man," Lydia asserted.

"And I'm four years older than him, remember?"

"Quack! Quack!" The duck jumped to the ground and stared at the two women.

"I agree with Puddleduck," Lydia said with a chuckle.

"Okay, I'll bite, what did she say?"

"Well, that was duck for *hogwash.*"

Molly smiled. Her mother seemed different since her accident. More outgoing and less inhibited. Molly liked the changes, but they took some getting used to. "I've never heard you use that expression before."

"Blame it on Puddleduck."

The duck glared at them accusingly, then waddled off to bed in the doghouse she used as a shelter.

"Four years," Lydia went on, "might have been important when you were sixteen and he was twelve, but it's not now. It didn't seem to hinder Clay tonight."

"I suppose you're referring to that stupid impulsive kiss?"

"Lord, yes." Lydia sighed dreamily. "When a man kisses you the way he did, and you kiss him back the way you did...well, let's just say that I didn't raise my girls to be kissing a man like that unless they meant it."

Molly could barely control her amusement. Her mother never discussed matters like this when they were younger. "I see. Clay was right about a mother's inherent need to matchmake."

"What do you mean?" Lydia asked, clearly confused.

"Never mind. Does Clay have a significant other, or is he waiting for Norma to find a suitable woman for him?"

"No one special. He thinks he wants to stay single. A crusty old bachelor is how he puts it. Of course, I don't believe a word of that."

"Why not?"

"Men just say that until they meet the right woman. Why, Joe was the same way, and you see how that turned out."

Molly sighed. "I've never seen two people more besotted with each other than Rachel and Joe. I'm envious of my own sister, isn't that awful?"

"But understandable." Lydia patted her knee. "Rachel owns a thriving real-estate business and she can work when the mood strikes. She's wildly in love with a wonderful man who just happens to love her back. And the two of them are expecting a baby in a few months."

"Yeah," Molly said softly. "Rachel has it all."

"All she had when she came to Morgan's Point was her career. She was suffering from the delusion that it was all she ever wanted. Morgan's Point has a lot to offer to anyone willing to take a chance."

"Mother, please don't get your hopes up. I'm really not sure where I'll end up, but it may not be here," Molly said gently.

"We'll just wait and see what happens." Lydia kissed her cheek. "I think I'll go back to bed."

"I don't want you to be hurt if I decide to move on."

"No, dear, I won't be." Her mother stood up and stretched. "But I would be mighty surprised."

Chapter Three

"You've only yourself to blame, Rachel." Molly whipped the potatoes with a vengeance. "If you'd told the truth in the beginning, you wouldn't be in this fix."

"I did." Rachel dumped a pan of string beans into a bowl that was too small and some of them spilled onto the counter. "Now, look what you made me do," she groused as she reached for a paper towel. "Wasn't that the doorbell? I'd better go see who it is."

"Oh, no, you don't," Molly said with a laugh as she handed her a larger bowl. "It's our job to get Sunday dinner on the table and you're not going anywhere. You're just trying to get out before I can ask you why you did it."

"Did what?" her sister asked innocently.

Molly groaned. "I could tell by the way people acted at the reception last night that you practically promised them I was coming here to be the new doctor."

"That's not exactly true. I told them you were still undecided and would make up your mind after you arrived. Can I help it if they assumed you're here to stay?"

Before Molly could answer, Lydia came into the kitchen with Clay. "Lay another place, Rachel. Clay managed to make it, after all."

"Like he's ever missed a free meal," Rachel said with a laugh as she sidestepped the dish towel he flicked in her direction.

"Don't pay any attention to her, Clay." Lydia checked the rolls browning in the oven. "You know you're always welcome here."

"I shouldn't stay. I need to go over some books at the store."

"Nonsense," Lydia told him. "Those books will still be there after you've had a decent meal."

"Well, if you insist." Clay leaned against the counter and looked at Molly. She was busy trying to avoid looking at him. The kitchen towel tied around her waist made him recall the strange dream he'd had last night. Although she was fully clothed now, Molly had worn only a frilly little apron in his fantasy and was baking cookies when she wasn't kissing him. He'd eaten his fill of the cookies, but he had been unable to get enough of Molly.

Normally he didn't remember dreams and was unsure if he even had them. This morning had been different. When he awoke his lips had felt swollen from imaginary kisses and he could have sworn he had a touch of heartburn from eating too many sweets. He didn't know what had prompted the dream, but it was certainly not based on reality. Molly was a career woman who had better things to do than bake. No doubt the dream contained some kind of Freudian message—or warning as the case might be.

He could take a hint, and this morning during his cold shower he'd made a decision. He would ignore silly dreams and stay away from the woman who caused them.

"Is your meeting over, Clay?" Lydia asked as she led him from the room. Members of the finance committee had met in an emergency session after church in an attempt to come up with an offer Molly could not refuse.

When Lydia and Clay left the kitchen, Molly flung the potato masher into the sink with such vehemence that soap suds splattered the counter. "I need to talk to Mom. Soon."

Rachel emptied the mashed potatoes into a serving bowl. "About what?"

"About trying to match me up with Clay. I won't stand for it."

"Mom and Norma Cusak have been trying to marry him off for years. It's gotten to be a habit with them."

"Well, it's a habit she's going to have to lose. If she expects me to stick around." Molly knew she was protesting too much, and the sly look on her sister's face confirmed it.

"Are you interested in Clay?" Rachel snitched a string bean and munched it.

Molly managed to appear appropriately insulted. "Of course not."

"I didn't think so. Besides he's too young for you."

"Only by four years." Molly frowned at the irritation her sister's comment caused. Hadn't she used that same argument herself?

"Uh-oh. Looks like I hit a sore spot." Rachel grinned. "Tell me what happened when Clay brought you home last night?"

"Nothing."

"You never could tell a lie, Molly. And you're a terrible bluffer. I can see by the look on your embarrassed face that something did happen."

"Nothing much," Molly amended.

Rachel shook her head. "I knew Clay was fast, but I didn't think he was that fast. Tell me, I'm dying to know."

"It was only a couple of kisses." She tried to downplay their importance for Rachel's benefit, but the memory of Clay's lips on hers revived feelings Molly would have rather forgotten.

"That good, huh?" Rachel smiled. "You have the most expressive face, Molly."

Molly knew she was caught, and denying it now would only make Rachel more persistent. She came up with a hurried excuse. "I've been at loose ends lately."

"Oh, call it what it is. You've been lonely, Molly. There's no shame in that. It's the spinster syndrome."

"That's ridiculous. And insulting, too."

"It's no insult. A man who reaches a certain age and is still unmarried is called a bachelor. A woman who attains that age and that status is called a spinster. There's nothing insulting about it. What would you prefer to be called—a bachelorette?"

"You know darn well society places an entirely different connotation on bachelor and spinster. Being a bachelor implies that the man has made a conscious choice about his life-style. Being a spinster implies that the woman would prefer to be married, but has no prospects."

Rachel shrugged. "I didn't coin the term. I'm merely pointing out that four years without male companionship is a long time."

Molly put her hands on her hips. "This may come as a surprise to you, little sister, but there are men in Montana. In fact, the male-to-female ratio is higher than in most states."

"So were you seeing anyone while you were there?"

"No."

"I rest my case. Four years," she shook her head in amazement. "No wonder Clay looks good to you."

"Clay would look good to most people," Molly pointed out dryly.

"That's true."

"And he knows his way around a kiss better than most. But I guess I'm not telling you anything you don't know."

"Well, actually, you are. Those brotherly pecks on the cheek and forehead never did much for me."

"Yeah, yeah," Molly scoffed.

"I swear." Rachel held up her right hand, then quickly dropped it again. "I take it back. He did kiss me. Once. But it was over almost before it started."

"Oh, sure," Molly said, disbelieving. It was only last night that she'd experienced those long slow caresses herself.

"No, really. He bloodied his lip on my braces and that was that. We decided the whole thing was over-rated."

"I think I agree. I'm not even sure why we're having this conversation."

Rachel took the rolls out of the oven. "Because you've given me something to think about. I never pictured you and Clay getting together. You've always been as different as chalk and cheese."

"That's right."

"But then, you know what they say about opposites attracting. Maybe it would work."

The sisters looked at each other and burst out laughing. In unison they exclaimed, "Not!" Molly was glad to discourage Rachel, but she was a bit hurt that she could do it so easily.

They bustled about, getting the meal together. At last Molly said, "It wouldn't work. When I fall in love, I want it all. Children, the works. Clay Cusak plans to go sailing off into the sunset in a few years."

"A few years could give you time to change his mind if you wanted to."

Molly shook her head. "He's a confirmed bache-lor. By choice," she emphasized.

Rachel munched another bean as she thought about it. "Determined maybe, but not confirmed. They make great husbands once they realize they can't live without you."

Molly smiled at her sister's new domesticity. "Spoken like a contented wife."

"Contented? Not me, not anymore. Content is what you are when you don't know any better. I was content with my life the way it was before. Why, I was so busy working and climbing the ladder of success, I didn't even realize what was missing in my life. Then along came Joe to fill up all the empty places."

"Speaking of empty places," Joe said from the doorway. "My stomach thinks my throat has been cut. We're starving out here."

Rachel picked up a bowl of food. "I was trying to explain to my sister that a career isn't going to keep her warm at night."

"It doesn't get all that cold in Florida, you know," Joe replied with a wink as he picked up a couple of bowls. "And contrary to popular belief, man cannot live on love alone. You can talk about marriage while we eat."

"No, we can't," Molly said vehemently. "Promise me you won't bring that subject up around Clay."

"It's a dirty job, but someone has to do it," Rachel declared with a perverse grin.

"Rachel . . ." Molly warned.

"Okay, okay."

Molly worried all through dinner about what her sister might say, but she kept her promise. Harmless small talk circulated the table, leaving her free to join in or quietly eat her food. She chose the latter. When she glanced up, she often found Clay watching her, but the only comments he directed her way were generic ones.

By the time dessert was served, Molly had convinced herself that the kisses they'd shared had meant little to Clay and were, in fact, only a momentary diversion. It was harder to tell herself that she didn't care.

Lydia served her a large slice of key lime pie. "I made this especially for you, Molly. It's always been your favorite."

"Thanks, Mom." The tangy aroma assailed her senses as she cut into it with her fork and made her tastebuds tingle with anticipation. It had been years since she'd tasted her mother's speciality.

"Looks delicious." Clay's eyes followed a forkful of the creamy confection to Molly's mouth. Then out of nowhere came the thought, accompanied by a loosening coil of desire, that it wasn't nearly as tempting as Molly herself.

He knew part of his interest in her stemmed from the fact that she had always been so aloof and disinterested in him. There were plenty of females willing to accept him on his own terms, so why was he having crazy dreams about one who was sure to want to change him? Molly was the kind of woman who would want it all. She'd never settle for the scraps of attention he was used to bestowing. So what was his problem?

Had he, like earliest man, succumbed to the lure of forbidden fruit? And if so, why didn't he learn from old Adam's mistake?

Clay was pondering these question when Rachel reminded him there were others present. "So how did the finance-committee meeting go, Clay?"

"Oh, fine," he said. Business was the farthest thing from his mind. He forced his attention on his own dessert dish and hoped his sweet tooth would distract him. Despite his best intentions, all he could think about was how yielding Molly's lips had been.

Shaking off those thoughts, Clay put down his fork and turned to Rachel. "I knew you and Joe were concerned—that's why I came by."

"Tell us what they came up with," Joe said enthusiastically.

Clay hesitated. "It hasn't been put to a vote yet."

"Aren't Earl Potts and the Dudley twins on the finance committee?" Lydia asked. When Clay nodded, she added, "Then it'll be all over town by morning anyway. Earl Potts is a bigger gossip than Bertie Caldwell."

"I'm sure the proposal will be passed—the deadline is getting close," Rachel said baldly.

"We're all council members, except Molly," Joe pointed out. "And since she's the one who'll be receiving the offer, she might as well hear about it now."

Clay turned to her. "Are you interested in hearing the proposition?"

Molly wanted to hear a proposition from Clay, but not the one he was talking about. Was it wrong to be selfish and put herself first for once in her life? She wished her family would let one day go by without talking about business. Still, she understood their concern about the town. She didn't want anyone to suffer because of her indecision.

At the heart of her reticence was the nagging worry that she would use the needs of her patients as an excuse to ignore her own. She'd substituted professional fulfillment for emotional fulfillment most of her adult life. It had happened in Montana, and it could happen in Morgan's Point.

"Come on, Molly," Rachel said. "It can't hurt to find out what they came up with, can it?"

It could, Molly thought, because she could easily get caught up in their enthusiasm. She could be persuaded to stay. She'd been here less than a week, and already she was fond of the town and its friendly people. Her family was here. And Clay. But was that a plus or a minus?

She glanced around the table at the expectant faces. "I'm listening."

The deal the finance committee had put together was more than tempting. If the town council voted in the proposal, and if Molly accepted it, she would receive a sign-on bonus to help her establish her practice. A portion of her fees would go into the general clinic account to cover overhead and other expenses, such as salaries for auxiliary staff. But if she agreed to stay ten years, she would eventually receive fifty percent ownership in the clinic.

"That sounds very generous," Lydia's husband said.

Lydia had tears in her eyes. "It certainly does, Ernie. And she could live right here with us. What could be more perfect?"

Before Molly had a chance to feel trapped, Clay went on, "That's another thing. When Doc Cooley died, he bequeathed his worldly goods and his house to Morgan's Point because he had outlived his whole family. Earl suggested we deed the house to Molly if she signs. As another incentive."

"That's a great idea," Joe said enthusiastically.

Lydia grinned at Ernie. "Good for Earl. When a man does nothing but sit in front of Wilbert's Hardware store all day, he's bound to come up with a good idea sometime."

Ernie returned her smile. "We do more than just spit and whittle, hon. We sometimes try to solve the problems of the world."

"That explains why the world is in the shape it's in," Lydia teased.

"The house doesn't look too bad, but it's pretty old," Rachel said. "I'll go over there and check it out this afternoon and see if it needs any immediate repairs."

"Didn't Doc have new wiring put in after the Jamisons next door had that electrical fire a couple of years ago?" Lydia asked.

"New plumbing, too," Ernie added. "I did the contracting for him. Saved him a bundle."

"There's no furniture. We auctioned it off to pay for Officer Hacker's gall-bladder surgery," Clay pointed out.

"I can help with that," Rachel said excitedly. "I'll just call in a few favors. I know some decorators who can get what she wants at cost."

The table buzzed with suggestions on how best to set up Molly's new home and organize the rest of her life. No one stopped to ask her what she thought, and after listening to the comments flying back and forth, Molly soon felt like a spectator at a tennis match. She let them carry on, careful to say nothing herself.

Despite their contagious enthusiasm, no one was going to railroad her into this. They could expound all day about decorating styles and structural soundness. She refused to make such a monumental decision without thoroughly thinking it through.

She glanced around the table and her gaze locked with Clay's. "What do you think, Molly?" he asked softly.

She was noncommittal. "As Mom pointed out, it's very generous. Almost an act of desperation, in fact."

"We never made a secret of that," Rachel said. "You know we're in a bind. Not only Morgan's Point, but all the surrounding communities who would use the clinic."

"Actually, a more accurate analysis would be that we're between a rock and a hard place," Joe put in. "But we don't want to put undue pressure on you."

"Of course not." Molly smiled at her family. They meant well, but she was starting to feel bamboozled.

Clay was torn between wanting what he knew was best for the town, namely, having Molly Fox head the clinic, and what was good for himself. If she stayed, he'd have to be extra careful not to let her ingratiate herself into his life. And the way he felt when he looked at her, he knew that was a definite possibility.

Just this morning, he'd had such good intentions where Molly was concerned. He would simply ignore her and all the unwelcome feelings she aroused in him. He would not let her get under his skin.

Sure. "Aren't you tempted?" he asked, his steady gaze giving his words a special meaning that the others at the table didn't notice.

"Yes," she whispered. By both offers. The one the town had come up with, as well as the one he made her when he looked at her like that. Was she the only one at the table who could feel the heat of his interest? Surely she wasn't so lonely that she would misconstrue his signals.

Clay Cusak was a dangerous man, and her heart would not be safe around him. And yet, a broken heart might be a small price to pay for the experience of knowing him for a while. Even if a lasting relationship was out of the question.

If she decided to stay, his plans would eventually take him far away from Morgan's Point. He'd been quick to tell her that. He obviously didn't want her, or any woman, to get any proprietary ideas about him.

Although she was no wide-eyed innocent, Molly had never really been in love. Over the years, she'd had short-lived infatuations, but she couldn't devote much energy to them and they hadn't survived long once the initial attraction wore off.

Not that she didn't believe in love. She did. She had great faith in its power and healing properties. As a doctor, she knew that patients who had the support of their loved ones did better than patients who did not. She'd seen some pretty miraculous things in her career, and because she claimed to be a scientist, she'd given those miracles the name science allowed them: spontaneous recovery. A scientific way of explaining the unexplainable.

But in her heart, in the part of her that would never succumb to rationality, she knew better. The real name for miracles was love. She'd seen it too many times.

And yet she was confused by these new and unfamiliar feelings. Her first reaction was to deny them, but she couldn't do that forever.

It was a hard habit to shake. As early as high school, Molly had realized she had to do something to discourage the males who were attracted to her. She feared that emotional entanglements at that stage in her life would interfere with her dream of becoming a doctor. Knowing she couldn't get into a good medical school with mediocre grades, she focused on academic achievement. Over the years it had become second nature for her to rebuff male advances.

Now she thought she might like to encourage those very advances. The problem was she didn't have a clue how to go about it. Her years of experience encompassed a very small area of her life: medicine. Flirting and other aspects of the male-female relationship were a mystery to her.

"Molly, dear," Lydia said, interrupting her tangled thoughts.

"What is it, Mom?"

"Rachel thinks you should have the house professionally decorated, but I think you should make your own selections...."

It was time to put an end to this. "I think you're all jumping to conclusions. The town council still has to vote, and I haven't said the magic word."

"Oh, yes," Lydia said contritely. "I suppose we just got carried away with hope. I'm sorry, dear."

"Me, too," Rachel added. "And we won't bring it up again."

"Thank you, I'd appreciate that," Molly said. But she knew they would if she hung around the house the rest of the day. "Now if you'll excuse me, I think I'll drive over to Lake Sampson for a while."

"That's nice, dear," Lydia encouraged her. "It'll give you a chance to think about things."

"Want some company?" Clay asked.

"I thought you had paperwork to do," she said, stalling.

Clay shrugged. "Never do today what you can put off until tomorrow."

Molly wouldn't do much thinking with Clay along, but neither did she want to be alone. She'd had four years of that. "Okay, let's go."

"Don't you want to change into something more comfortable, dear?" Lydia asked.

Molly looked down, surprised to see that she was still wearing the dress and pumps she'd worn to church. "Yes, I suppose so."

"So do I," Clay said as he slid out of his chair. "I'll be back in ten minutes."

Thirty minutes passed and Clay still hadn't reappeared. Determined not to wait, Molly walked outside and climbed into her Blazer. It still bore the dust from her cross-country drive and contained the accumulated debris of the fast-food meals she'd consumed en route. Just as she started the engine, Clay pulled in beside her.

She sat there, the engine running, while he climbed into the passenger seat.

"Sorry I'm late." Molly didn't answer, but she fastened her seat belt. He took that as a good sign.

"I don't normally keep a pretty woman waiting, but I have a good excuse," he said as they backed out of the driveway. "Want to hear it?"

Molly glanced at him and noticed the gleam in his blue eyes. "Not really. I was having second thoughts about going with you, too."

"That's not what kept me. Officer Hacker gave me a speeding ticket and a twenty-minute lecture. That's his favorite part. He paints a disgustingly lurid picture of exactly what happens to human bones at the moment of impact.''

Molly laughed in spite of herself. "Rachel warned me to watch out for him. She said he gave her one the first week she was in town.''

"He's a good man and he takes his work seriously and I respect that." Clay added with a to-hell-with-it grin, "But let's forget about him and all things serious.''

"All right.''

"Let's devote ourselves to the pleasure of the day.''

"What's that supposed to mean?" Molly was definitely having second thoughts about being alone with Clay.

"Nothing," he said innocently. "Just that it's a beautiful spring day. We should enjoy it. That's all. Were you thinking of some other kind of pleasure?''

"No, I wasn't. It'll be nice to relax. I haven't done that in a long time.''

"Things were pretty rough for you in Montana, weren't they?''

"Why do you ask that?''

He indicated the road she should take before answering. "I just figured it had to be tough being responsible for the health of all those people.''

"The toughest part was knowing what I couldn't do. There's a lot wrong with the reservation system, but it took me a while to realize I couldn't fix it. All I could do was try and make sure the kids got their vaccinations and tell pregnant women how important it was not to smoke. I could dispense medicine and stitch up knife wounds, but I couldn't really change anything.

Native Americans have a beautiful and historic culture. Poverty and oppression are also part of the legacy."

"You kept it from overwhelming you," he said.

"Barely." She saw the Lake Sampson turnoff and drove the Blazer down the narrow blacktop road. "Believe me, there were plenty of times when the problems of the world seemed too much for Molly Fox."

"Don't underestimate your power to do good. Anyone who cares as much as you do has to make a difference in the lives of the people you know."

"Why, thank you, Clay." Molly was genuinely touched by his sincerity. "Considering that you don't know me very well, I take that as a compliment."

"Oh, I think I know you better than you realize."

Chapter Four

The lake, surrounded by tall pine trees, was calm in the sultry afternoon heat. April might mean early spring in some states, but in this part of Florida it heralded summer. Clay directed Molly to the boat dock where he kept his small sailboat, and it only took them a few minutes to launch it. Few other boaters were out and Clay explained that he liked this part of the lake for that very reason. He didn't like riding other people's wakes.

They tacked aimlessly for half an hour in the gentle breeze, then Molly watched as Clay took down the spinnaker. He'd discarded his T-shirt and she couldn't help admiring the muscles that rippled across his back while he worked. His movements were graceful and practiced, with no wasted motion. He was at home on the water and looked at ease with a boom in his hands.

His skin was bronzed and shiny, and she was seized with a sudden yearning to touch him. She wondered how he'd react if she did, then quickly reminded herself that she was alone with him in the middle of a nearly deserted lake. She knew exactly how he'd react. The only smart thing was to keep her hands to herself.

Still admiring his body, Molly leaned back against the deck cushions and debated the question that kept popping into her mind. Mainly, could Clay Cusak give her what had been missing in her life?

It was true that his kisses transported her into schoolgirl giddiness and his touch was strangely electrifying. He made her laugh and he was easy to be with. But there was a price to pay for all that. He wasn't the marrying kind, and he could potentially give her more pain than joy. Molly was understandably confused. She was new at playing with fire and didn't know all the rules.

Clay's task finished, he stretched out beside her. "The wind is completely gone. There'll be no thrilling race across the lake today."

"Are you disappointed?" she asked.

"No," he said lazily. "I'm always content on the water."

"I read in the paper this morning about the Fourth of July Cup race. Are you entering?"

"No, I'm not the competitive type. I leave racing to those who have something to prove." He raised himself on one elbow. "I've been told that's a major flaw in my personality."

Molly turned onto her stomach and rested on her elbows. "Did a woman tell you that?"

"No, the dean of my college. He called me in to explain that if I really applied myself and brought up my grade point, I could graduate in the top two percent of my class."

"And did you?"

"I was already in the top ten percent, and all that extra studying would have interfered with my weekend sailing." He grinned at her. "What do you think?"

"I think you went sailing."

"Why do I get the feeling you disapprove of the choice I made?"

"I don't, not really," she denied. "I just wonder why."

"I went to school on a full scholarship and held down a part-time job for spending money. The week was a drudge of study and work, and those weekends were my reward for the good grades. Why should I have punished myself by giving them up?"

"But weren't you the least bit curious to know if you could have made it?"

"I'm sure I could have. But why beat out some poor devil who had no other reason to live?"

Molly laughed. "I see you're arrogant, as well as irresponsible."

"Do you think so?" he asked seriously. "I just know my capabilities and my limitations. I'm not out to prove anything to anyone."

"Not a bad philosophy."

"Thanks." Clay sat up. "Let's go for a swim."

Molly shook her head. "Are you crazy? The water's too cold this time of year."

"Come on. The sun's hot and will warm us up fast."

She sat up, wrapping her arms around her knees. "Sorry, I didn't bring a suit."

Clay grinned. "Neither did I."

"If you think I'm going skinny-dipping with you, you *are* crazy," Molly said vehemently. The thought was titillating, but she would never seriously consider it.

"You always did lack a sense of adventure," he said easily as he slipped out of his shoes. "We'll wear our skivvies. The only difference between swimwear and underwear is the fabric and the price."

Embarrassed, Molly turned her back when he unzipped his cutoffs, and she didn't turn around again until she heard the splash from his dive. She leaned over the side of the boat and watched the spot where he'd gone in.

When he came up for air, she asked, "What are you going to do for dry underwear, silly?"

He tossed back his hair and cold drops of water splattered her. He grinned at her in that way he had. "I'll go without. It may be a novel idea to you, but there are societies that have never even thought of wearing clothes under their clothes."

"There are also societies that don't wear clothes at all," she reminded him. "But that doesn't mean I'm going to give it up."

"Come on in, Molly," he wheedled. "The water's fine."

"And fifty degrees."

"Nah. It's at least sixty-five."

"I really shouldn't."

"But you want to, don't you?"

She was sorely tempted. It wasn't rational and it wasn't smart, but she wanted to fling herself into the water and right into Clay's strong arms for as long as he cared to hold her. And she wanted to do it without thinking about whether it was right or wrong and without worrying about the consequences.

"Then do it," he said, treading water. "For once in your life be spontaneous."

"Maybe I'm too shy." She was frantically trying to recall what kind of underwear she'd worn today. Was it the white cotton industrial-strength variety? Or the wispy revealing kind? And which did she want it to be?

Clay turned his back to her. "I'm going to count to ten and you'd better be in the water or I'm coming after you. I'll throw you in, clothes and all. One."

Molly knew he was serious and she didn't want to explain to her family why she came home soaked. She quickly unbuttoned her blouse and sighed with relief. Her lingerie was at neither end of the continuum. Her bra was a modest satin underwired affair and no more revealing than a bikini top.

She kicked off her shoes. "Tell me the water isn't cold."

"I'm as warm as an Eskimo sitting by a fire," he said glibly. "Four."

Molly skinned off her jeans. Her matching high-cut briefs were equally demure. "What happened to two and three?"

"You used them up with your silly questions. Six."

"Six?" Molly exclaimed, perched on the edge of the boat. "Maybe you should have given up a weekend or two in your youth for remedial math classes."

"Ten," he yelled, and was answered by her splash as she jumped into the water.

She came up gasping and laughing. "You liar! It's freezing."

"It's a little chilly, but you'll get used to it," he called as he swam to the boat.

"Don't you dare leave me out here, you dirty rat. I'm shivering so badly I doubt I can swim back to the boat."

"Keep moving," he advised. "It's warmer that way. I'll get you a life jacket."

Molly kicked and paddled and grudgingly admitted he was right. Movement did indeed help her body adjust to the numbing cold. When he swam up to her, she saw he was wearing a ski vest. He helped her into the other one and wrapped his arms around her.

"Are you warming up?" he asked, their noses nearly touching.

"You lied to me," she accused. "You said it was warm."

His eyes sparkled with mischief, and she recalled that he'd looked much the same way when he was an ornery twelve-year-old. "No, I didn't. How warm can an Eskimo be by a puny little fire, surrounded by all that ice?"

"You've got me there," she said softly.

"No," he whispered. "I've got you here. Right where I want you."

"You do feel kind of warm," she conceded.

"I've wanted to kiss you all day," he said in a husky voice.

"When I was eating key lime pie," she guessed.

Clay nodded. And that was only the start of it. He'd never wanted a woman more. He couldn't figure it out, and he wasn't going to waste time analyzing it now. The feeling was all that mattered. "The whole time I was sitting there calmly answering questions about the finance-committee meeting, I was secretly wanting to do unspeakable things with that meringue."

The moment his lips touched hers, throbbing with a passionate message that matched her own, a strange heat flowered inside her. Her body washed into his with a bone-melting warmth, and they lost themselves in quick-breathing eagerness.

Clay tore his lips from hers. "We'd better get back on the boat and dried off before we catch colds."

"Don't worry," she said against his lips. "I'm a doctor. I know what to do."

It was dark by the time they got home. Clay pulled her into his arms and kissed her good-night on her mother's front porch.

"I'm sorry I coaxed you into the water," he said when she turned away from him to go inside.

She paused on the threshold. "I'm glad you did."

Clay sneezed and they laughed. "I think I'm catching a cold, Doc."

She smiled at him. "Take two aspirin and call me in the morning."

The next day Molly's throat was a little scratchy, so she gargled some saltwater, and that helped some. However, by the time breakfast was ready, she had developed a runny nose. She drank the orange juice

Lydia thrust at her and went back to bed without a fuss.

A few hours later, her mother poked her head in the door. "Good, you're awake. Hattie Benson brought you a pot of her homemade chicken soup. Said it was just the thing for a cold. Want me to bring you a bowl?"

"No, I'll get up. I am hungry and I feel a lot better." Molly padded into the kitchen and sat down at the oak table. "Who's Hattie Benson, and how did she know I had a cold?"

"She runs the lunch counter and soda fountain at the drugstore," Ernie said. "I don't know how she knew you were sick, though."

Lydia grinned. "Did you mention it to Earl Potts when you went down to Wilbert's Hardware this morning?"

"I might have," Ernie said. "You ready to go? The bridge tournament at the seniors center starts in thirty minutes."

"You go without me," Lydia said. "I'll stay with Molly."

"Mom, don't be ridiculous. You and Ernie have been talking about this tournament for days. I'm fine."

"Well, all right. After all, you're the doctor. But if you need me, you call. The number is on the pad by the kitchen phone."

After they left, Molly ate the delicious soup. She was just about to cut herself a piece of pie when the doorbell rang. When she answered it, she found Miss Watkins, the home-ec teacher, on the porch.

"I heard you were feeling a little under the weather, dear, so I made this for you." She handed Molly a German chocolate cake. "Sweets always make me feel better, don't they you?"

Molly clutched the front of her bathrobe together and smiled. There were no medicinal properties in cake, but she thanked Miss Watkins graciously. "Won't you come in?"

"Oh, I can't stay. I've got my little poodle Coco in the car, and we're on the way to the doggie salon. Besides, you should be resting. Rest is very important to healing. But you probably already know that, being a doctor and all. Starve a fever, feed a cold, isn't that what they always say?" she asked without giving Molly time to answer. "Enjoy the cake, and I hope you'll be feeling better soon."

"Thanks again, Miss Watkins. But you shouldn't have gone to so much trouble."

"Oh, it was no trouble. Just being neighborly. I enjoy baking, and the folks in Morgan's Point take care of each other."

Her words turned out to be prophetic. Molly had just returned to the kitchen when the Dudley twins stopped by to give her a deck of cards, saying that solitaire would keep her from getting bored while she recuperated. She invited them in for cake, but they shyly declined. She should be resting, they told her.

Molly was well into her second piece of the dessert when Mrs. Perkins stopped by with a gallon of ice cream from her ice-cream parlor, claiming it would go just right with German chocolate cake.

Her next unexpected visitor was Bertie Caldwell, a flighty little woman who also declined Molly's invitation to come inside. She brought Molly a gaily wrapped package and insisted she open it immediately, saying, "It's a useful gift. Nothing fancy, mind you. I always try to give something useful. I embroidered them myself. Ladies can never have too many hankies."

"Thank you, Ms. Caldwell," Molly called to the woman's hastily retreating back. She sneezed and put Bertie's gift to immediate use.

Molly went to the kitchen, put on some water to boil and found a box of herbal tea bags in the cupboard. While she was waiting for the kettle to whistle, she thought about Morgan's Point. It was a lovely unspoiled place, full of old-fashioned down-to-earth people who had a special beauty all their own. They were friendly, caring and giving. She could do a lot worse than to make her home here.

Taking her cup of tea to the front porch, Molly settled in the wicker rocker thinking she would soak up a few of the sun's rays for a little while. The brain-pounding beat of heavy-metal music blared from the driveway, and she walked around the house to investigate.

She stood there in her bare feet and bathrobe and watched as a group of teenagers noisily hosed down her dusty Blazer.

"Hello!" Molly called over the din.

A pretty blond girl of about fifteen stepped forward. "Hi, my name's Heather Benson. Like, my mom works at the drugstore and everything. You must be the new doctor."

"I'm *a* doctor," Molly corrected.

"That's Mike and Larry Hacker." The girl motioned to the two lanky adolescent boys who wore their baseball caps backward and their shorts baggy.

Mike and Larry raised their hands in acknowledgment and squirted soap over the car. An ocean of excessive suds appeared and ran down the driveway.

They were obviously not experienced car washers, but Molly waved at them. She was still unsure if theirs was an act of hospitality or vandalism.

"They're Officer Hacker's nephews from Lake City," Heather said in a whispered aside. "They're spending the summer here because their folks are getting a divorce."

"I see," Molly said, even though she didn't.

"You know how boys are," Heather went on confidentially. "I thought it would help keep them out of trouble and cheer them up a little if we washed your car."

"They certainly look happy now," Molly agreed. The two boys had turned the hose on each other and the soapy vehicle was temporarily forgotten.

"Mom says idle hands are the devil's workshop or some such thing. And the best thing to do when you're feeling sorry for yourself is to do a good turn for someone less fortunate."

Molly grinned. "Less fortunate?"

"Well, you're sick and we ain't, so that makes you less fortunate, right?" Heather tossed her blond hair.

"But I'm not really sick. I just had a case of the sniffles this morning. I'm fine now."

Heather's delicate brow scrunched in thought. "Can we wash your car, anyway? These guys need something to do. And I kind of like spending time with them."

"Sure, but it's pretty grimy from traveling across country. I'd be willing to pay if you do a good job."

"Oh, no! You can't pay. That ain't how it works around here," Heather explained patiently. "All you have to do is say thanks, and then you do us a favor when you can."

"I see," Molly said. "Thank you."

"You're welcome, Doc. But just one more little thing—you really ought to go sit on the porch or something. And maybe try to look a little sicker. It'll make the boys feel better about the whole thing."

"You got it." Molly walked back around the house, still smiling at the ingenuousness of the girl. She sank back into the rocker and picked up her cup of tea. She almost choked when a Jacksonville florist's van pulled into the driveway.

A middle-aged man hopped out and sprinted toward the porch with an embarrassingly large spring-flower arrangement. "Molly Fox?"

"Yes," she said, wondering which local citizen had gone to so much trouble and expense, all because they'd heard through the grapevine that Dr. Fox had a cold.

"Then these are for you." He set the flowers on the porch, handed her the card and left as quickly as he'd come. Molly looked at the elaborate bouquet and had a strong premonition about who'd sent them. Her hand shook as she ripped open the envelope.

Next time we decide to strip down to our underwear, I promise the conditions will be warmer. I

accept full responsibility for your illness and promise to make it up to you.

Clay.

Heather, Mike and Larry sauntered around the house and over to the porch. "Got some flowers from Jacksonville, huh?" the plucky little blonde asked.

Molly stuck the card in her pocket. If Clay went to the trouble to send her flowers from out of town, he evidently wanted to keep gossip to a minimum. "Yes. Aren't they lovely?"

The boys shrugged and discovered their shoes.

"Boyfriend?" Heather said knowingly.

"Family friend," Molly countered.

"Oh, then they're from Clay," Heather informed the boys.

"He's cool," Mike informed Larry. "But why did he send you flowers if you're not his woman?"

Molly changed the subject. "You know, boys, if that soap dries on the car, it'll streak and have to be done all over again."

Molly smiled when the kids raced back to their task. She carried the flowers inside and put them on her bedside table before calling Clay.

"Cusak's." There was no mistaking the masculine voice.

"Hi, this is Molly."

"Hi. How are you feeling?"

"Special," she said. "The flowers are beautiful. Thank you."

"You're more than welcome. I feel like a heel for luring you into the lake. I shouldn't have done that."

"I'm glad you did. I had a great time. It was a first—the most fun I ever had while contracting an illness."

"Maybe it won't be the only first for us."

Molly was silent for a moment too long. She knew he knew what she was thinking. She started chattering about all the other nice things people had done for her that day.

"Yeah, we're real friendly folks in Morgan's Point," he said.

"Especially when you want something."

"Look at that bunch of flowers again, Molly. You'll notice there are no strings attached." Clay's voice had taken on a hint of coolness.

"I'm sorry. That wasn't very gracious of me. I didn't mean to imply that all those wonderful people had ulterior motives."

"Good. Because they don't. However, I can't make the same claim."

"Oh?"

"I was hoping the flowers would make you realize what a nice guy I am."

"And?"

"And if you feel up to it, maybe you would like to have dinner with me tonight. I could show you around town. Give you the grand tour."

"How long would that take?" she asked.

"Hmm. About fifteen minutes. Twenty, if I show you the famous tree."

"You have a famous tree here?"

"Oh, yes. It's not to be missed."

"In that case, I don't see how I can possibly refuse."

Chapter Five

For dinner, Clay took Molly to a seafood restaurant out on the highway. The specialty of the house was all-you-can-eat deep-fried shrimp, served with huge platters of french fries and hush puppies, and bowls of creamy coleslaw on the side.

Clay was obviously a regular, and everyone seemed to know and like him. Everywhere he went, he generated goodwill and warmth among those he met. Molly felt fortunate to be the one he'd singled out for his attention. He was unique. He was the only man she'd known who could wear khaki slacks and a chambray shirt and look dressed up, somehow adding his own brand of elegance to the most casual attire.

The other customers waved and called greetings from across the dining room. The high-school girl who seated them thanked him for catching the error on her grandfather's heart-medicine prescription. After taking their order, the middle-aged waitress asked him to recommend an over-the-counter remedy for her son, who had caught a spring cold.

Later, the cook came out of the bustling kitchen with a fresh plate of shrimp and asked Clay's opinion on what care he should give a nasty blister from a splatter of hot grease.

"Maybe you'd better ask the lady, Ralph," Clay said. "She's the doctor." Although she didn't look much like one tonight. She was very appealing in a white ruffly blouse that dipped low enough to reveal the shadow of her cleavage. Her long gauzy indigo skirt hid the shapely legs he well remembered from the day on the boat. Her shoulder-length hair was loose and casual, and she wore Gypsy-style gold rings in her ears.

The big man in the white apron must have questioned her credentials because he appraised Molly skeptically. "You really a doctor?"

"Yes, sir, I am."

"Good enough. What should I do about this here burn?" He thrust his injured hand in her direction.

Molly examined the quarter-sized burn where a blister was already starting to form. "Soak it in cold water until the burning stops."

"Should I put some butter on it?" he asked.

"No, that'll only trap the heat and make the burn worse. Wrap it in a clean dry cloth and don't put anything on it for twenty-four hours. Then you can start using an antibiotic ointment if you want."

"Thanks, Doc." The man seemed satisfied with her recommendations and lumbered back to the steamy kitchen.

"Is it always like this?" she asked Clay.

"Like what?" he asked innocently.

"You know what I mean."

"If you decide to stay here, you'll have to get used to it. You can't stop being the doctor just because it's after hours."

"How well I know that. People don't always get sick between 8 a.m. and 5 p.m." Molly helped herself to more shrimp. She usually tried to limit the amount of fat and fried foods in her diet, but tonight she was making a delicious exception. And while she was in the mood, if Clay wanted to make her the kind of proposition she usually rebuffed, she might make an exception for that, as well.

He leaned across the table and caught the flowery scent of her hair. He wanted to stroke the silky mane, but this was not the place. He'd have to touch it before the night was over. "Would it be premature for me to ask if you've made a decision about Morgan's Point yet?"

"No. I'm still trying to make up my mind." Molly nibbled a piece of crispy shrimp. "What made *you* come here?"

He waited for the waitress to refill their iced-tea glasses before answering. Normally Clay didn't care to reveal facts about himself to the women he dated. But he was comfortable sharing personal details with Molly, perhaps because of their past association.

"When I finished pharmacy school, my mother moved here to be near Lydia. While I was visiting, I heard the drugstore was for sale and went to check it out.

"I'd inherited some money and liked the idea of being my own boss. I made Mr. Threadwell an offer and he accepted it. The business had been going downhill for several years, and I wanted to see if I could turn it around."

"So you did. Does everything you touch turn to gold?" She wondered what she would turn into if he touched her. If past experience was any indication, it would be something in the quivering category.

He laughed and resisted the testosterone-prompted urge to bask in her praise. "Hardly, but hard work does pay off in the long run. It was a simple matter of giving the customers what they needed so they wouldn't have to go elsewhere."

"I get the feeling that in a town like this it's essential the people accept an outsider. Was that ever a problem for you?"

"Not really. Your mother paved the way for me. Everyone liked Lydia, and if she said I was okay, then I was all right with them."

"Folks have been very good to me since I've arrived."

"They really need you here, Molly. But they like you, too. You won't have any trouble fitting in."

Molly accepted the compliment and noticed he was more serious than usual. His uncharacteristic demeanor made her nervous about what the rest of the evening might bring.

When they'd consumed all the shrimp they could, Clay suggested they return to Morgan's Point for an evening walking tour of the town. Since cars were banned from the main square, he parked the pharmacy van on one of the side streets.

"It's like stepping back in time," Molly said. They strolled along the wide sidewalks and admired the window displays in quaint stores like the Hobby Horse Toy Shoppe and the Stylish Boutique. A couple of times she thought he was going to hold her hand, but he seemed to change his mind at the last minute. She became more nervous, but tried not to let it show.

"People around here want to keep it that way," Clay told her. He had a hard time concentrating on the friendly conversation; he was already anticipating the good-night kiss.

"So I've heard."

"Joe's a very protective mayor. I guess you know all about how he and Rachel locked horns."

She laughed. "Oh, yes. Mom told me Rachel wanted to bring in outside developers, and Joe opposed her."

"That's putting it mildly. Joe fought her tooth and nail. It was something to see. Fortunately Rachel finally saw the light."

"I'm glad. There aren't many places like Morgan's Point left in this country. It would be a shame to change it."

They came to an old-fashioned flower vendor on the corner. An elderly black man wearing a straw hat and denim overalls sat on a little stool beside a cart filled with brightly colored flowers.

"How's business, Abraham?" Clay asked.

"Not bad, Mr. Clay. Not bad at all. Been a good spring for flowers."

Molly sniffed some of the extravagant blooms, and Clay selected a bunch of white daisies. He presented them to her with a flourish.

"Pretty flowers for a pretty lady." The old man flashed an approving grin as he accepted payment from Clay. "You made a good choice, Mr. Clay."

"The lady? Or the flowers?"

"Why, both, suh."

"Thank you, Abraham."

"Thank *you*. Ya'll have a nice evenin'." Abraham tipped his hat and they walked on.

Molly buried her nose in the bouquet. "I don't think I've ever received flowers twice on the same day before." She would enjoy this simple reminder of their evening together as much as she had enjoyed the elaborate florist's arrangement he'd sent earlier. She wouldn't admit it, but it had been a very long time since anyone had cared enough to send her flowers.

"Abraham looked like he could use the business," Clay said dismissingly in an attempt to downplay the gesture. The truth was he'd never given flowers to the same woman twice in one day before, either. But he liked to please Molly, and her pleasure was all the reward he needed.

At dusk the Victorian street lamps came on, and Molly commented about the unique architectural design of the buildings in the downtown area.

"The town's early settlers were transplanted New Englanders," Clay explained. "I believe the original Morgans came from New Hampshire. They built a town like the ones they'd left behind."

Molly nodded approvingly. "It's a refreshing change from the Spanish-influenced styles of the coastal areas."

They heard the unexpected strum of a banjo coming from the little park in the center of the square.

Clay finally took Molly's hand and led her to the source of the music.

"A bandstand!" she exclaimed. "I didn't know such things still existed."

"It's a popular spot here in the summer, and not just for concerts. Politics get debated from the bandstand, and a few people have held weddings here."

The whitewashed structure was the focal point of the park. Members of a five-piece bluegrass group were tuning their instruments under its gingerbread-trimmed roof.

"Hey, Huey!" Clay called out to the man with the banjo. "What's up?"

"We're just practicing for the Bluegrass Festival next month. Stick around and give us a listen."

A small group of spectators had gathered by the time the group began playing the old familiar tunes. Some sat on the park benches, and others made themselves comfortable on blankets spread on the grass. Children laughed and chased fireflies. Old women called to them to be careful before going back to their gossip. Little knots of men discussed the weather, and mothers bemoaned the fact that in a few weeks school would be out for the summer and then what would they do with the kids?

"I really do feel like I've walked through a time warp," Molly told Clay. "Only it's a time I know little about, because I wasn't around then."

"That's what I like about Morgan's Point," he said. "Life is much simpler here. It's almost possible to forget that the rest of the world is in turmoil when you're surrounded by so much tranquillity."

Molly looked around and smiled at the friendly people who waved and called out greetings. The demands of the city seemed far away. She could find a peace and fulfillment here that had eluded her in the isolation of the reservation.

"Let's go," Clay whispered as he tugged on her hand. "We can stop at Perkins's for ice cream before we drive out to the Trader's Oak."

"How did a tree get to be so famous?" she asked later between licks of her chocolate-almond ice-cream cone. They had driven to the outskirts of town and Clay had stopped the van on the side of the road. He pointed out a tall lone oak tree some distance away among the pines.

Clay was momentarily distracted by the pink tip of her tongue on the creamy chocolate, but he managed to pick up the thread of the conversation. "It was the site of the earliest trading post in this area. One of Joe's ancestors came to Florida back in the early 1800s. I believe his name was Micajah Morgan, but Joe could tell you more about it than I can."

"He's quite proud of his heritage and the fact that his ancestors were among the first white settlers in the area, isn't he?" she asked.

Clay nodded. "Joe has a deep appreciation of history and the part his family has played in it. It's a unique heritage he'll pass along to his and Rachel's children."

Molly thought about the baby her sister carried. How lucky it would be to have a father who was bound to a place by blood ties. The child would have roots. It would belong because it was a Morgan and would never have to search for its place in the world.

He put his arm along the back of her seat and leaned close, touching the corner of her mouth with his fingertip.

"What?" Her breathlessness revealed more about the state of her emotions than she wanted him to know.

"You have some chocolate on your lip." He was tempted to get even closer but, afraid of where that might lead, resorted to his usual diversionary tactics. "I've never found women with mustaches very attractive."

Molly laughed nervously. She was filled with both disappointment and relief. "Let's get out of the van."

The moon had risen and the evening air was balmy and inviting. They leaned against the side of the van and listened as unseen insects generated a night music all their own.

"It's lovely out here," Molly said with a sigh as she looked out at the pine forest. "So quiet."

"Yes, it is." Clay was totally confused by his reaction to Molly. He usually didn't back away from the normal progression of things physical, and he didn't know why he was doing so now. All he did know was that he couldn't treat her as lightly as he had other women.

It was easier to discuss facts than to think about feelings. "Joe worked for a long time to get Cypress Knoll declared a protected wildlife refuge. It's now under extended lease to the government. Next month, the forestry service will start building camping and hiking areas. More people will be able to enjoy the natural beauty of the place."

"Rachel told me how she'd almost made the biggest mistake of her life," Molly put in. Clay had fallen back into the role of tour guide. Would she ever get used to the mercurial nature of his moods?

"The Margolian Brothers?" He didn't try to conceal his contempt for the development company that had tried to take over the property for their own greedy purposes.

"Yes. She said their idea of progress was to destroy every living thing, pave it over and build shopping malls."

"That'll never happen here. With any luck, and Joe's continued vigilance, Morgan's Point will always be as old-fashioned and behind the times as it is right now."

Molly was glad the town would remain untouched, but she was well into mourning her own untouched status. She'd been anticipating Clay's kiss all evening. He'd had several opportunities—she'd seen to that—but he hadn't taken advantage of any of them.

"You seem genuinely fond of the town and the people here," she said.

He looked at her oddly. "I am."

"So why are you leaving?"

"That'll be a few years down the road," he replied, hedging.

"But you'll go eventually."

"Yes." Clay didn't sound as sure as he once might have. Since meeting Molly, he'd begun to question the wisdom of leaving a successful business, his family, friends and a comfortable old age for the uncertainty of an unencumbered life in the Keys. Maybe that was why he felt so confused.

What were the words to that old Janis Joplin song? 'Freedom's just another word for nothin' left to lose." Was that true? Did he believe it? He wasn't sure anymore.

"You were always such an adventurous child," she told him. "Maybe you grew up and settled down too soon, before you got the urge to roam out of your system."

"Maybe that's it. I know I don't want to end up like my father."

Molly knew Walter Cusak had died unexpectedly. Just as her own father had. She and Clay had that in common. "In what way?"

"He worked nearly forty years for the same company. He gave up weekends and vacation time so he'd have plenty of money saved up for his retirement. I was the only child, and I was born relatively late in their lives. When I was a kid, I'd ask my dad to play ball with me or take me fishing."

"And?"

"He was always too busy. Said he'd have time for all that when he retired. He postponed his life, and then he never got to enjoy the retirement he saved for."

"I'm sorry, Clay."

"You lost your father, too."

"Yes. But I was so wrapped up in medical school that it was several years before I really missed him. I wish now I could go back and live some of that time over again."

"But we can't do that, can we? We never get a second chance at life. That's why I don't want to stay in Morgan's Point and wonder what might have been. At the risk of sounding like a beer commercial, I want to grab all the gusto I can.''

"And you have to sail off on a boat to do that?" she prompted.

"That's the way it looks right now."

Molly tried not to think about what might happen if she decided to stay in Morgan's Point and let her feelings for Clay get away from her. She would be hurt when he left, that much was sure. What she didn't know was what she should do about it.

Should she stop seeing him now as a protective measure against future pain? Or should she adopt his attitude and try to experience it all while she could?

"It's getting late," she said. "Maybe we should go." She made no move to go back into the van and continued to stare up at the star-filled sky.

"I was just thinking the same thing." Clay stayed where he was. He was well aware of the fact that he was all alone with a beautiful woman, far enough away from the rest of the world to avoid any potential interruptions. He wanted to take her into his arms, but for the past few days he'd waged an internal debate on the matter of Molly. It wouldn't be wise to get involved with her. Yet he didn't know if he had the strength of character to do the wise thing.

"Do you believe in fate?" she asked unexpectedly at his side.

"I think things happen for a reason," he allowed. "I don't know about fate."

"I'm beginning to think I was fated to come to Morgan's Point. Of all the places in all the world where I could have gone, I ended up here. I'm a doc tor, and the people of this town badly need a doctor. That's not just a coincidence, is it?"

He appeared to consider her question. "It could be. But if it is, it's a coincidence named Lydia and Rachel."

She laughed. "I guess you're right. They did engineer the whole thing."

A slight breeze picked up and the evergreens soughed softly in the night. Clay turned to Molly and, as he gazed at her lips, doing the wise thing became impossible. He pulled her into his arms. "There's one thing you'll learn if you stay in Morgan's Point, Doc."

"What's that?" She had a hard time getting the words out, so badly did she want him to kiss her.

"I'm almost always right."

"Is that so?"

"You've been standing there for the past ten minutes or so looking at the stars and talking about fate. But what you've really wanted to do was kiss me."

Molly was suddenly embarrassed and was grateful for the darkness that hid the flush creeping up her neck. She tried to step away from him, but he held her close. "So are you a mind reader, too?" she demanded in her haughtiest voice.

"No. But I'm right, aren't I?"

"You're always right, remember?"

"That's what I thought."

His lips came down on hers without further delay, brushing them lightly, almost hesitantly. They were gentle and warm, undemanding. She relaxed and his arms tightened around her, pressing her soft curves into his unyielding chest. Molly's skin was highly sensitive to his touch and she responded with abandon.

His mouth worked insistently, opening her lips to his exploring tongue. Her arms went around his neck and she clung to him, her body melting into his as the world receded and was replaced with an exquisite physical arousal.

His hand slid up and down her back, and warm pleasure washed over her like a wave. No man's kiss had ever affected her in quite the same way; she was intensely aware of the heat of his body, of the hard muscles under her hands, of the spicy scent of his cologne. She felt like a teenager, kissed for the first time and newly awakened to the wonders of passion.

His lips drew away from hers reluctantly. "That was really something, Doc," he whispered. "You put a whole new twist on this kissing business."

She smiled. "So, I guess it was as good for you as it was for me."

"If it was any better, you'd have to administer CPR."

Molly laughed. "Twenty years ago, if anyone had told me that someday I'd be standing in the moonlight kissing Clay Cusak, I'd have punched him out."

"Not me," he said with conviction.

"Really?"

"I told you—I've always had a crush on you, Molly. Why do you think I tried to make your life so miserable all those years? It was the only way you'd pay any attention to me."

She didn't quite know how to respond. "You certainly know how to get my attention now," she said uneasily. She was embarrassed that she'd practically thrown herself at the man, and he knew it.

"Maybe I should take you home."

"That would be a good idea."

They drove back to town in silence. When Clay parked the van in front of her mother's house, Molly turned to him. "I don't understand my feelings toward you, Clay. Like they say in the old movies, 'It happened so fast.' But given your future plans, and the unsettled nature of my own, perhaps it would be a good idea if we didn't let things get out of hand. Maybe we shouldn't see each other so much."

He was quiet for a long moment, the only sound the tapping of his fingers on the steering wheel. He didn't look at her when he said, "No."

"No?"

"No. That is not acceptable. I don't want to give up seeing you. I don't understand my feelings, either, Molly, but I don't want to run away from them."

"It's not a question of running away from anything," she argued. "It's a question of being careful."

"You're the one who brought the subject of fate up in the first place," he accused. "Maybe we're fated to spend as much time together as we can. Who are we to tamper with destiny?"

She looked at him carefully. "You're kidding, right?"

"Am I?"

"I hope so."

"I'll call you tomorrow." He restarted the engine.

"Good." She reached for the door latch. She'd never been smart where Clay was concerned.

"Sweet dreams." He kissed her again. Thoroughly.

"Good night." She climbed out of the van, aroused, frustrated and certain that her dreams that night would be anything but the sweet variety.

Chapter Six

"Come on, Molly," Rachel urged. "The supplies and equipment for the clinic have arrived, and Joe and I need your help."

Molly looked up from the medical journal she was trying to read. She'd come out onto the porch to enjoy the cloudless spring morning. And to escape her sister, whose relentless wheedling session was only loosely disguised as a visit. "What do you need me for?"

Rachel perched on the arm of Molly's chair, slipped the magazine from her hands and flipped it shut. "We need your professional expertise to help us unpack and set things up."

"Who would you get to help if I weren't here?" Molly knew she was being manipulated, but the fact didn't particularly bother her. After spending time with her mother, her sister, her brother-in-law and the other citizens of Morgan's Point she was getting used to it.

"Oh, in that case—" Rachel sighed dramatically "—we'd have to stumble along in our own clumsy way." Then she brightened. "Fortunately we don't have to do that. We're lucky enough to have you."

"You don't have me yet," Molly reminded archly. The town council had been patient, but she would have to give them her answer soon. Normally assured and decisive, she couldn't seem to make up her mind about Morgan's Point. In the three weeks she'd been here, she'd grown fond of the little town and its friendly self-sufficient citizens.

Despite her reservations, they'd welcomed her wholeheartedly and given her their trust and respect. They'd wooed her and treated her like visiting royalty. It felt good to be so important to people.

So why was she holding out? She liked the idea of being near her family, of attending her sister's delivery when the time came. There were special rewards in being part of a close-knit community where she could make a real difference in the lives of its people. And yet she wanted to consider an outside offer. An offer she hadn't mentioned to anyone else.

If she was to draw up a list of pros and cons regarding Morgan's Point, she would undoubtedly have a long column of pros. As far as she could tell, there was really only one major con to be considered. His name was Clay.

Despite her efforts to avoid the inevitable, she was falling in love with him. They'd been together a lot during the past couple of weeks, seeing each other whenever they could. Since the evening they'd visited

Trader's Oak and Clay had told her he didn't want to stand in the way of fate, they'd been sailing twice, but both times they'd kept their clothes on and stayed on the boat. They'd been out to dinner several times, gone into Jacksonville to a play and generally hung out together.

As much as she tried to tell herself that they were just friends, that she simply enjoyed his company, Molly knew it wasn't true. She cared about Clay Cusak in a way she'd never cared about another man. And someday he would leave Morgan's Point, and then where would she be?

She was almost thirty-five and ready to settle down. She wanted a home of her own, family, children. The last thing she needed at this stage in her life was to have her heart broken by a footloose bachelor whose idea of domestic bliss was living on a boat.

Rachel interrupted Molly's thoughts by giving her a big hug. "I wish you'd hurry and make up your mind. You will stay, won't you? I never realized how much I'd missed you until you came back. And it would be so good for Mom if you were close. She won't say anything, but she's missed you, too. She's been so happy since you've been here."

"I guess the fact that she has a new husband and is about to become a grandmother for the first time has nothing to do with it?"

Rachel shrugged. "Maybe. But she needs us, Molly, now that she's getting older."

"Please." Molly laughed. Since Lydia had recovered from her accident, she was probably the least decrepit grandmother-to-be she'd ever known.

"You *have* been gone a long time...." Rachel's words trailed off in what sounded suspiciously like an accusation.

Molly retrieved the journal and held it in front of her face in mock defense. "Don't try to lay more guilt on me, little sister. It won't work."

"It's Clay, isn't it?" Rachel asked with dead-on accuracy.

"What's Clay?" Molly pretended not to understand the abrupt change of subject, but was impressed by her sister's perceptiveness.

"He's the reason you're waffling about this. Damn." Rachel crossed her arms under her bosom and paced around the porch. Judging by the look on her face, she was torn between loyalty to her friend, love for her sister and plain old self-interest.

"Clay has nothing to do with it," Molly declared. She hated being dishonest, but she wasn't ready to discuss her feelings about Clay Cusak. Not even with Rachel. She didn't understand them herself yet. "It's a big decision, one that will affect the rest of my life. I just want to be sure I make the right choice."

"No fair fibbing, Molly." Rachel plopped down in her stepfather's rocking chair, her hands resting on the slight mound of her belly. "Let's talk straight. Clay's a charmer and I love him like a brother. But take my advice, sis. Don't pin any hopes on him."

"I'm not planning to."

"Good. You know, two or three years ago, you might have had a chance at domesticating that wild hare. He was a little more settled then, more predictable. But he's changed. He's not the same old Clay I've always known."

"Maybe you're the one who's changed, Rachel."

"No, it's him. He's got his heart set on that boat thing, and he's just stubborn enough to make it work. When he takes a notion, he can be the most focused person I've ever met. The only surprising thing was that he came here in the first place."

"What do you mean?" Molly liked to take advantage of any chance she got to gain insight into Clay.

"When we were kids, he always talked about how he was going to travel and see the world when he grew up."

"I remember," Molly said with a smile. "You called him Captain Adventure."

"For a good reason."

"I guess even gadflies have to land somewhere."

Rachel elaborated. "Morgan's Point is a place where you end up when your gadding days are over, after you've had it with the rest of the world. It's no place to start from."

"I think buying the pharmacy and working to make it successful was exciting in its own way to Clay. At first. Now that it's no longer a challenge, he's losing interest." Molly wondered if he'd lose interest in her, too, if she ever let him know how much he'd come to mean to her.

"That might be part of it. But I think it has to do with hitting thirty. That's a major turning point in a man's life. Maybe he's decided that if he's ever going to do all those things he used to talk about, he'd better get started."

"You're probably right. You know him better than anyone else." Molly doubted that she would ever understand him.

"That's right, I do. I know you shouldn't sit around moping over a man who doesn't have the good sense to realize how much he'll be giving up if he leaves. Base your decision about the job on what's best for you, Molly. Don't even try to factor in Clay Cusak. He's an uncertain element."

"I'll keep that in mind." Molly attempted some enthusiasm. "Well, come on, we'd better get moving if we're going to get all that stuff unpacked today."

Rachel jumped up, a self-satisfied smile on her face. "You mean you'll help?"

"Did you ever doubt it?"

"Not really."

"I thought not. Even if you don't know a hypo from a hemostat, you must have realized that I couldn't resist the temptation to set up a brand-new clinic."

Rachel's grin turned smug. "I was counting on it, anyway."

The two women met Joe at the clinic and the trio spent the rest of the day unpacking cartons and checking invoices. Molly was impressed by the quality, and quantity, of the equipment they'd ordered. As she put away the supplies, she couldn't stop thinking about using them to ease pain and save lives. In her very own clinic.

"You made some excellent choices, Joe," she commented. "How did you know what to order?"

"I didn't. Clay set me up with a very conscientious salesman at the medical-supply house. He gets the credit."

"And the commission," Rachel interjected.

Examining an autoclave used to sterilize instruments, Molly said, "This model is state of the art."

"I told you this is going to be a first-class clinic," Joe reminded her. "That's why we want you."

She stacked boxes of tongue blades in a supply cabinet before turning to her sister and brother-in-law. "There's something I need to tell you."

"Finally!" Rachel sighed. "I thought you'd never accept."

"You've decided to stay on with us?" Joe prompted.

Molly wasn't sure how to break her news. She'd kept it to herself for three days, hoping it would get easier to share. It hadn't. "Not exactly," she said.

"So, what is it, sis?"

"I got a phone call the other day from Barbara James, an old friend from my residency days. She's an established family practitioner in Palm Beach now."

"And?" The note of suspicion in Rachel's voice only made Molly's job tougher.

"She's so successful, in fact, that she's expanding her practice."

"And?" Now it was Joe's turn to be suspicious.

"And when she heard I was back in Florida, she called."

"You said that already," Rachel put in.

"She wants to talk to me about a partnership."

"Molly!" Rachel's disappointment was pure and undiluted. "I hope you told her to forget it."

"Actually, I said I'd come down to Palm Beach to see what she had to offer."

"Oh, Molly, you didn't." Rachel paced around the room before whirling on her sister. "I can't believe you'd go behind our backs."

"I'm not going behind your backs," Molly protested. "I'm telling you up front. Before I even go."

"But to accept another offer! I just can't believe you'd be so heartless."

"I haven't accepted anything yet. I just think I need to be damn sure of what I want before I decide."

Tears filled Rachel's eyes. "I thought you *were* sure. I thought family might finally mean something to you. I guess I was wrong." She headed for the door.

"Rachel, wait a minute. Can't we talk about this?" Molly felt helpless in the face of her sister's anger.

"No! Joe, I want to go home." She didn't slam the door as she left, but the silence made a statement just the same.

Molly turned to Joe. "I'm sorry. I didn't mean to upset her so much."

He patted her shoulder. "Don't worry about Rachel. This pregnancy's made her very emotional. She'll get over it."

"I hope so."

"Of course, we'll all be disappointed if you decide to go elsewhere. But we'll try to understand." Joe looked around the sparkling clinic with regret. "With any luck, we'll find another doctor before the government deadline," he added without conviction.

"Et tu, Brute?"

"What?"

"If you're trying to make me feel like a rotten heel for checking out other possibilities, you've succeeded."

"I don't want you to feel badly, Molly," Joe assured her. "But I don't want to lose you to Palm Beach, either. If it's a question of money, I might be able to work out a more advantageous deal with the council."

"No, Joe. The deal you offered is generous enough." Unreasonably Molly felt that she'd somehow betrayed a trust. Yet, she knew she was doing the right thing. "How will I know if Morgan's Point is the right place for me if I don't know what other places are out there?"

"You're right. Of course." He squeezed her hand and gave her a key. "I should see about Rachel. Will you lock up when you leave?"

"Sure." Molly watched him go. He stopped at the door.

"I know you'll make the right decision in the end, Molly."

She smiled reassuringly, but she didn't feel half the conviction she pretended.

She went back to her work; organizing the supplies helped keep her mind off Rachel's reaction to her announcement. And it kept her from worrying that maybe she should have rejected Barbara's offer out of hand.

As she moved about the clinic, Molly imagined it staffed and in full operation. She knew just how she would set up the triage for maximum efficiency, something she'd learned on the reservation. With the help of a good office manager and some dedicated nurses, Morgan's Point Clinic could be a model of quality health care. As its only doctor, she would provide essential services that the locals now had to go to

Jacksonville to receive. And she would have only herself to answer to. It was a heady thought.

She was considering appropriate decor for the waiting room when she sensed a presence in the room. She turned and found Clay watching her from the doorway.

"Surveying your kingdom, Doc?" he asked with a grin.

She hoped he didn't notice the incriminating flush that crept over her face. She'd been doing exactly that—having covetous thoughts about the clinic. "I was just giving Joe and Rachel a hand with the supplies."

"So they said."

"You talked to them already? They only left here a few minutes ago."

He shrugged. "Bad news travels fast and all that. Besides, Rachel was so upset about your impending trip to Palm Beach, nothing short of a cherry phosphate would soothe her."

"And you came charging down here to add your two cents' worth, I presume."

"Actually I came charging down here to see if I could further riddle you with guilt and self-recrimination for having the unmitigated gall to commit such a traitorous deed."

"Thanks a lot."

"Anytime." He perched on a stainless-steel counter and folded his arms across his chest. "So let's hear your side of the sordid story. Tell me exactly how you plan to pull the rug out from under the poor people of Morgan's Point."

Molly made no attempt to hide her exasperation. "For heaven's sake, Clay. Must you be so melodramatic?" And why did he have to be so physically exquisite, too? she wanted to ask. As a doctor, she had an acute appreciation for perfectly formed human specimens. And Clay, dressed in modishly casual slacks and a crisp white shirt, was as close to perfect as she'd ever seen.

Just looking at him, recalling the breathless wonder of his touch, the burning torture of his practiced kisses, very nearly made her giddy. And that annoyed her. Women her age were not supposed to become giddy by merely thinking about a man. It wasn't mature and it sure as heck wasn't smart.

"Well, Benedict Arnold, how do you plead?" he persisted.

"If you must know, I'm going to see an old friend in Palm Beach. Barbara James has expressed an interest in having me join her medical practice. End of story, and it's not sordid at all. I don't know what all the fuss is about. I haven't said yes yet."

"But you didn't say no. Some might construe such actions to indicate a possible maybe."

"So what?" Molly was getting tired of explaining herself all the time, and her irritation was evident in the clipped question.

Clay slipped lightly off the counter and strode to her side. She wished he'd keep his distance, because his nearness only made it harder for her to think straight.

"See, the problem is you've also told us maybe. That's kind of like having two dates for the prom, Molly. Who are you going to dance with? The one who gives you the biggest corsage?"

"May I assume by this line of questioning that you are in agreement with Rachel and Joe?"

"I'm disappointed that you would consider another offer, yes."

His arm brushed hers and a little arc of awareness leapt between them. "What do you care? You're not going to be here much longer yourself."

"That's true. But my family and friends will be. I'd rest easier knowing they were getting good medical care."

"While you're off wandering the bounding main and avoiding responsibility," she added.

"While I'm in pursuit of happiness," he corrected her with a grin. "According to the constitution, I'm allowed to do that."

"But I'm not?" she demanded.

He rolled his eyes. When he spoke, his words had the artificially soothing tone of a rational person explaining something to a totally irrational one. "You'd be much happier here than you would in Palm Beach. Everybody knows that. Besides, it's the principle of the thing. You have a duty."

"The people in this town are not my responsibility," she insisted. "Not yet, anyway. I never promised anyone I'd stay. And until I do—"

He reached up and brushed an errant strand of hair from her cheek. "Oh, but you have stayed. For three whole weeks. If you didn't like it here, you should have said so and left a long time ago."

His touch had an instant galvanizing effect on her. All her senses zeroed in on that one tiny spot, and she unconsciously leaned into him. "I've been visiting," she protested weakly.

His fingertip drew a light line along her jaw. "You've been toying with us, Doc. You've taken advantage of our need."

"I have not." She could barely get those three words out, much less accuse him of doing the same thing.

He lightly circled her lips with his finger. "You've been leading us on when all the time you had another offer waiting in the wings."

Molly felt the adrenaline start to pump through her blood. Her pulses quickened and her stomach tightened. A curious warmth spread through her veins. Oh, he was good, all right. She'd been physically aroused before, but never in such a slow deliberate manner.

If he didn't do something soon, if he didn't kiss her and release some of the tension mounting inside her, she would have to take drastic action.

"No," she said, sounding more breathless than she liked. "I only spoke to Barbara three days ago."

He leaned closer and Molly could feel the heat of his body. She could smell the crisp scent that was uniquely his: soap and antiseptic, spicy cologne and a hint of cherry flavoring. "So what are you waiting for?" he asked in a husky demanding voice.

Molly didn't know if he was talking jobs or kisses, so she went with her gut reaction. She took his face between her hands and pulled his lips down to hers. She briefly considered telling him he needed a shave, but she decided to save her breath. If this kiss was anything like the others, she'd need it.

In all honesty, Clay couldn't say that he was surprised by Molly's actions; after all, he'd been goading her in that direction since he'd first stepped into the clinic. But he was impressed by her fervent lack of subtlety. It supported his theory that it was carefully tended fires that burned hottest.

He didn't believe in letting the lady do all the work, and he contributed to the event in his own way. The kiss and all its associated choreography went on for a long time, but Molly grew limp before he was ready for it to end.

"You tricked me into doing that," she accused in a shaky voice, which was apparently the best she could find.

He feigned innocence. "I did not. I merely came in here to try and reason with you, and before I knew what was happening, you attacked me. Which, I might add, you may feel free to do at any time. Except in the presence of children, the elderly or anyone with a heart condition."

"Dammit, Clay, can't you be serious for five minutes?"

"I thought the last five minutes were pretty darn serious. At least you kissed me like you meant it. I hope you weren't just taking advantage of the situation."

"What situation?"

"Oh, you know. I come to you humbly to plead my case, to beg if necessary to keep you from leaving. That automatically puts me in a vulnerable position. We're all alone in the sexually charged atmosphere of a sterile medical office, surrounded by all manner of potentially stimulating objects." He looked askance at the big box of fluffy cotton balls on the counter and raised his eyebrows suggestively.

She pushed him away with a laugh. Clay had a real talent for diffusing a "sexually charged atmosphere" with his well-timed wit. She suspected he used it much as an animal used protective coloring for camouflage.

"You're crazy," she told him. "And if you weren't so damned cute, I wouldn't give you the time of day. Now get out of here and let me finish my work."

He stepped close and grasped her by the shoulders. He looked into her eyes with studied concentration.

"What?" she demanded warily.

"I'm trying to be serious, Doc. Don't spoil the moment."

"Clay—"

"Look, Molly, I understand why you want to check out the prospects in Palm Beach. I really do. Frankly, I don't blame you. You owe it to yourself to explore every opportunity."

"Thank you. Your permission means the world to me," she said lightly.

"But while you're down there talking fiscal earnings and profit margins, remember that money can't buy happiness."

"Unless you have a lot of it and spend it all on yourself," she said. "In which case it can come darn close."

"I know you better than that. You didn't get into medicine for the money. You care about people. Maybe you care too much. That may be your problem."

She wanted to slip out of his grasp, but then she'd have to contend with the awful emptiness she'd feel when they parted. "The problem is a whole town full of folks who think they know what's best for Molly Fox. And you're one of them."

At that moment, for a split second, Clay knew exactly what he wanted to be. Not just one of the people who loved Molly. The one who loved her most. The thought of leaving her suddenly seemed like the dumbest idea he'd ever had, and he couldn't even remember why he was planning to go. He had to keep reminding himself about freedom, independence and living the good life.

"Find out what your friend has to offer," he said quietly, his lips close to her ear. "Just don't forget what you could have here."

His words made Molly's heart jitter as if it had been zapped with a defibrillator. Would he always have that unsettling effect on her? "You know, Clay, when you stop with the jokes and wisecracks, you give pretty good advice."

"I do, don't I?" He planted a quick kiss on the end of her nose before starting for the door.

"Yeah," she chided under her breath. "You should try following it sometime."

Chapter Seven

Two days later Molly left her Blazer at the Jacksonville airport and caught a commuter flight to Palm Beach. Barbara James met her plane, and the two old friends caught up during the drive to the clinic. They'd scheduled the visit after office hours, and Barbara gave Molly a tour of the facilities, introducing her to the other two partners, a young husband and wife.

Molly complimented them on the sleek understated elegance of the decor. The rich carpets, signed lithographs and plush furniture spoke of prosperity. The children's waiting room was decorated in bright primary hues and filled with colorful toys and appealing artwork.

"Our practice sees patients from cradle to grave," Barbara, a svelte blonde, commented. "Rob is a pediatrician and Katherine is a board-certified gerontologist. I take care of everyone in between. We have full caseloads—in fact, none of us are accepting new patients right now. That's where you come in," she added with a smile.

"What about referrals?"

"Not that we need them at the moment," Barbara said with a wry expression, "but we have a good working relationship with the internists and cardiologists in the building. We all have admitting privileges at two of the local hospitals, and we try to maintain a high profile in the community. We keep a public-relations firm on retainer for that purpose."

Molly wanted to question her friend further, but Barbara explained that they would discuss the business end of things over dinner. They just had time to drive to Barbara's condominium and change. Reservations were at seven at one of the most popular restaurants in Palm Beach, where they would meet Rob and Katherine Cox.

Molly had always made it a practice not to discuss business while she was eating, but apparently the other doctors had no such qualms. They trotted out facts and figures, supposedly to impress her with the financial solvency of the clinic.

She tried to enjoy the delicious dinner, but it seemed to Molly that the three ambitious young doctors were overly concerned with profit margins, volume billing and the high cost of malpractice insurance, which they tried to recover by operating an in-house laboratory.

She assumed that because there was a lab in the clinic, the doctors probably ordered unnecessary and costly tests. Barbara told her that she'd have to become intimately familiar with Medicare and third-party insurer's policies to make sure that no claims were denied.

"We don't take welfare or indigent patients," Rob pointed out. "We've found that it's bad business."

"What about their health care?" Molly asked.

"Oh, there are other doctors in town who will see them. Or they can go to the county hospital."

Molly thought the bespectacled young man displayed a cavalier attitude toward those less fortunate. That phrase struck a familiar chord and she recalled what Heather Benson had said about feeling better when you could help others. Obviously Palm Beach and Morgan's Point were separated by more than miles.

"Each partner is expected to bill a certain amount each month," Barbara went on. "Everything over that earns a bonus."

"So, if you're a workaholic like your friend here," Katherine put in, "it could be quite a profitable business for you."

"There are only so many hours in the day," Molly said.

"We have an excellent office staff who pyramids our appointments. Even if one or two cancel in any given time slot, there are others to fill it," Rob explained.

"I've never liked overscheduling. The patients have to wait too long and it's an inconvenience to them," Molly said softly.

All three doctors looked at Molly as if she'd just said something totally subversive.

"Patient convenience is not our primary concern," Barbara said coolly. Obviously she'd heard the censure in Molly's words.

"What about quality of care?" Molly asked. "How much time do you spend with each patient?"

Rob laughed, but it was uneasy. "As little as possible."

There were some very important questions Molly needed to ask. "How do you begin the visit with your patients?"

"What do you mean?" Barbara asked.

"Do you spend a few minutes chatting about how their lives are going, or do you get right to the point?"

The three looked at each other, wondering if it was a trick question.

"I usually ask the patient how I can help him," Katherine said. "What's wrong with that?"

"What do you do when the patient offers information that might change or influence your diagnosis?" Molly persisted.

The three looked confused. "I think we're getting off the subject." Barbara pulled a folder out of her briefcase and spread it on the table. "Here's what we can offer you, Molly. Let's take a look at some figures. I think we can all agree that we didn't spend twelve years in training to become philanthropists."

By the time the check arrived, Molly's mind was made up. Not only about Palm Beach, but about Morgan's Point. Barbara's offer was very attractive, but Molly knew she couldn't practice the kind of high-tech volume medicine they had chosen. At one time, she'd thought that was exactly what she wanted, but now she knew better.

She was interested in people, not in profit. Sure, she'd made that crack about money buying happiness, but that was for Clay's benefit. She realized now that there were different kinds of riches. She would consider herself wealthy indeed if someday the people of Morgan's Point talked about her in the same hushed reverent tones they used when discussing the many qualities of the late Dr. Cooley.

Although she'd often protested to the contrary, Molly had long suspected she wouldn't be happy with the anonymity of a big-city practice. Acquisition of the trappings of success could make a young doctor forget why she'd gotten into the field in the first place. While she didn't begrudge Barbara and her colleagues their kind of medicine, it simply wasn't her style.

And that's what she told her friend, as gently as she could.

"I think you're making a big mistake," Barbara told her as she drove to the condominium for Molly's bags before taking her to the airport. Molly had originally planned to stay the weekend, but now she was ready to go home.

Home? Was that what Morgan's Point had become in her mind? In only three short weeks? Suddenly her heart felt lighter than it had in a long time. She experienced the spirit-lifting certainty of someone who knows she's doing the right thing.

"No, Barbara," she told her friend. "I respect what you and the other doctors are doing here, but it's not for me. I don't look at sick people and see dollar signs."

Barbara laughed. "I should probably take offense at that remark, but I won't. We've been friends too long."

"Thanks for understanding."

"So, tell me about Morgan's Point."

And Molly did, in lengthy and loving detail. She told her about the people, the Trader's Oak, the quaint shops on the square. She told her how fulfilling it would be to live in a town so long that she delivered the babies of babies she'd delivered.

"I want to grow old there, Barbara. And be Old Doc Molly, a curmudgeonly spinster who knows all the dark secrets of everybody in town. What power that will give me," she said with a laugh.

Barbara let her out at the airline gate and leaned across the seat. "You might grow old, Molly Fox, but I'd bet my next year's bonus check that you won't be curmudgeonly. Or a spinster."

Having gotten in late the night before, Molly was still asleep the next morning at nine. She awoke to hear someone pounding furiously on the front door. Recalling that her mother and stepfather had left the day before to visit Ernie's sister in Orlando, she grabbed her robe and was tying it around her waist when she threw open the door.

A very excited young man stood on the porch. "Oh, thank God, you're here, doctor. I'm Ray Johnson. My boy's been stung by a bee and he's real sick."

Molly was instantly alert. "How long ago?"

"Less than an hour ago. We didn't think much of it. I mean, kids get bit by insects all the time."

"Come in while I throw on some clothes." Through the bedroom door, she called, "How old is your son?"

"Three."

Molly got a sinking feeling in her stomach as she rushed back into the living room less than three minutes later. "Any history of allergic reaction?"

"He never got stung before," the poor father said, close to tears. "He's having trouble breathing."

"Where is he?"

"Outside in the car with Betsy. We were heading for the emergency room in Jacksonville when I saw your Blazer. Lucky for us you were here."

Molly grabbed her medical bag, ran outside and hopped into the back seat where a distraught young woman was cradling a dark-haired little boy in her arms. The child was conscious, but just barely. The sting site on his arm was swollen and had turned a vicious red.

"Get us to the clinic as fast as you can," Molly ordered Ray who threw the transmission into reverse and backed out of the drive at top speed. The old car roared off in the direction of the clinic. Molly took the child from his mother and positioned him flat on his back, with his legs raised to improve blood flow to the heart and brain.

"What's wrong with Timmy?" Betsy cried. "How could something like a bee sting do this to him?"

"Timmy's had an allergic reaction to the insect venom, which has caused anaphylactic shock," Molly explained. "This kind of hypersensitivity is rare, but it can be dangerous."

"Will he be all right?" Hysteria had crept into the mother's voice.

"As soon as we get to the clinic, I'll give him an injection of epinephrine. In most cases, that's enough to stop the reaction."

Betsy was still crying when they reached the clinic. Molly raced ahead to unlock the door and set up the supplies she would need. Ray ran into the examination room with Timmy in his arms. Betsy followed, sobbing openly.

"I think he's stopped breathing, doctor," Ray said, his voice tight with panic.

"Oh, my God!" Betsy cried. "Help him! Do something!"

In seconds, Molly was administering cardiopulmonary resuscitation. She hadn't mentioned how life-threatening anaphylactic shock could be to a child Timmy's age because she hadn't wanted to frighten the distressed parents any more than they already were. But she knew she was running out of time, and she put all other thoughts out of her head. She concentrated on the small body that responded to her ministrations, and worked calmly and efficiently to save his life.

Once Timmy's breathing and heart rate were reestablished, she prepared a hypodermic syringe with the medication to counteract the allergic reaction. Within minutes of the injection, the child's color had improved and he was breathing easier.

For the first time, Molly looked up from her patient. "He's going to be all right now," she reassured his parents. "It was a close call, but we got him here in time."

"Thank you, Doc." Ray pumped her hand, tears streaming down his face. "Thank you for saving my boy."

Betsy hugged her. "He wouldn't have made it to Jacksonville, would he, Doctor?"

Molly knew she had to be honest with the young parents, even if the truth was painful. "Probably not. He had a severe reaction. You did the right thing by bringing him to me." And she had made the right decision when she left Palm Beach early and returned home ahead of schedule. Fate had helped her save this little boy's life by insuring that she was in the right place at the right time.

"I'm so glad we've got a doctor in Morgan's Point now," Ray said. "Folks'll just rest easier knowing you're here."

"So you will be staying with us, Dr. Fox?" Betsy asked hopefully.

Molly smiled as she stroked her young patient's head. He was beginning to come around and his dark eyes looked up at her questioningly. He didn't understand what had happened to him, but he seemed to know he was in good hands, because he smiled back at her. It was a weak smile, but it meant the world to Molly. She felt as if she'd just been given a wonderful gift.

"Oh, yes," she told the Johnsons enthusiastically. "Wild horses couldn't drag me away now."

She kept Timmy at the clinic for several hours for observation and then sent him home with his parents. She gave them a preloaded syringe of epinephrine and showed them how to use it in case Timmy was ever stung or bitten again. She also recommended they take the child to an allergy specialist in the city who could help them understand Timmy's problem and teach them ways to cope with it.

After the Johnsons left, Molly sank into the big comfortable chair behind the desk that would soon be hers. Before she could call Joe and tell him her decision, the door to the clinic flew open and Clay rushed in.

"I just heard about Timmy Johnson," he said.

She shook her head. "I'll never get used to how fast news travels in this town."

"You saved his life." The awe in his voice was apparent.

"I'm a doctor, Clay. That's what I'm trained to do."

"He wouldn't have survived the thirty-minute trip to Jacksonville. He would have died if you hadn't been here."

She looked at him and, for the first time during the trying morning, tears filled her own eyes. "Yes, I think he might have. He had a very severe reaction."

Clay rushed to her side and pulled her into his arms. "Thank God you came back, Molly."

She rested her head on his shoulder and allowed his strength to seep into her. She hadn't realized how drained she felt until now.

"Surely you realize now how much the people of Morgan's Point need you, Molly," he whispered into her hair.

She did know. The town needed her as much as she needed Morgan's Point. She needed a place to call home. A place to belong. She wanted to watch Timmy Johnson grow up, knowing she had been a part of the miracle of life. She knew now that she could more easily give up practicing medicine altogether than she could be part of a busy, impersonal big-city practice.

He held her at arm's length. "Wait a minute. I thought you were spending the weekend in Palm Beach. Why did you come back so early?"

"Fate?" she suggested humbly.

A wide smile crept across Clay's face. "You made your decision, didn't you?"

"Yes."

He was quiet for a long moment. "You are going to stay, aren't you?"

"How could I not?"

He hugged her tightly and buried his face in her hair. "What made up your mind?"

"I realized after talking to Barbara and her partners that I wasn't cut out to practice their kind of medicine. They keep a public-relations firm on retainer," she said with amazement.

"And that's why you came back early?"

"I wanted to get home," she said quietly.

"You made the right decision, Molly. You won't ever be sorry you chose to stay here."

"I know." She hoped he would never be sorry that he chose to leave. She knew she could fulfill her professional potential in Morgan's Point, and she was at peace with that. She wasn't so sure about the emotional side of her life. What would that life be without Clay? He didn't understand that it was just as important to be needed by a single person as it was to be needed by a whole town. Even if that person didn't need her.

She wanted to tell Clay she had fallen in love with him. But that wouldn't be fair. He'd made it clear from the very beginning that he would leave Morgan's Point someday. As much as it would hurt, she would have to let him go. Because she did love him, she didn't want him to make any sacrifices for her that they both might live to regret. Because she loved him, she would make it easy for him to leave.

She slipped from his arms and walked around to her desk. "I guess I should call Joe and give him the good news."

"He's probably heard by now, but go ahead and call him. Make your sister a happy woman so she'll quit banging on my door in the middle of the night crying for cherry phosphates."

Molly laughed, but she didn't feel nearly as light-hearted as she sounded. "Thank you for being my friend, Clay."

He sat on the corner of her desk. "Oh, is that what I am?"

"I hope we can be friends. We can still go out and have fun, but I think we need to remind ourselves that we can't let our hearts get involved."

Clay tensed. Had he misread her signals so completely? When he'd held her in his arms earlier, she'd felt like anything but a friend. "I don't understand, Molly."

"There's no point in playing games, Clay. Now that I've made my decision, we have to face facts. I'm going to be in Morgan's Point for a long time. You can't wait to leave. As soon as your proverbial ship comes in, your ship will sail out."

"And?"

"And I think it would be foolish for us to get too deeply involved."

"More deeply than we already are, I assume," he said coolly.

"I'm not the kind of woman who takes romance lightly," she told him. "I don't think I can have a love-it-and-leave-it relationship."

Clay wasn't sure where she was taking the conversation. "Am I correct to assume that you do not want to have a short-term affair with me?"

She flinched at the bluntness of his words. "I think that's a fair assumption."

"So when can I see you again?"

"Clay! Haven't you heard a word I've said?"

"How about dinner tonight?"

"I'm sorry, I can't."

"Tomorrow night?"

"Clay, give me some time, okay?"

"Okay," he agreed reluctantly. "But don't take too long."

Over the next few days, Molly dealt with Clay as she'd always dealt with distractions—by pretending detachment. Her family was thrilled and the town council was ecstatic about her decision to accept their offer. Plans were made for her to take occupancy of Doc Cooley's house, and she ordered necessary repairs and painting.

Molly threw herself into her new job and soon hired a nurse and office staff. Before long, Heather had been hired to help answer the phone. As word of her medical skills spread, mostly by Timmy Johnson's parents, she got down to the business of doctoring. She was so busy she hardly had time during the day to think about Clay. When she did, she felt a sadness that they would never truly know what they might have meant to each other.

She arrived at the clinic every morning by seven to review patient files before seeing her first patient at eight. During the first couple of weeks she mostly treated spring colds, allergies, earaches and other routine illnesses. She was called on to stitch up a farmer's leg and to set a teenage boy's broken arm.

Mary, her new nurse, suggested she might like to set up health screenings at the elementary school, and that project led to the establishment of an immunization clinic for infants and toddlers. Molly had very strong opinions about immunization for children and was gratified with the positive response from the community.

As word spread about the new doctor, people started coming in from surrounding towns and rural areas. Within a few weeks appointments were at a premium, but Molly instructed her staff not to turn anyone away who required medical attention. She would extend the clinic hours if necessary, but she would see everyone who needed to be seen.

Because her house was still undergoing repairs, Molly collapsed on the bed in her mother's spare room at the end of each long and full day. She was tired, but filled with the knowledge that she had provided the people of Morgan's Point with much needed services. She no longer worried about fitting in. The residents of the town had accepted her with open arms, chocolate cakes and homemade preserves.

One benefit of her busy schedule was that it made it possible for her to avoid Clay without seeming to do so. She instructed the office personnel to tell him she was busy when he called, unless it was of a professional nature. She spoke to him occasionally, usually when he had a question about a prescription she'd written. A few times she'd had to call him to inquire about the side effects of a certain medication, but she never let the conversation get personal.

The evenings were a different matter. He often stopped by her new house to help with the renovations. She was careful to be gracious and grateful for his assistance, but she made sure they were never alone. It was hard to maintain an emotional distance from Clay when it was the last thing she wanted to do. The strain of pretending she didn't regret the change in their relationship, coupled with her busy schedule at the clinic, exhausted her.

She was so tired and so busy she could almost convince herself she wasn't lonely. Almost. In truth, she missed Clay, even though she saw him frequently. It was painful to care for someone and have to treat him like a casual friend. She could still laugh at his jokes, engage in teasing banter with him, but she missed the closeness they'd shared. She missed his kisses, his warmth and understanding. He had to know what she was trying to do, but he was too stubborn to acknowledge the fact that she was closing the doors between them.

For that she was grateful. She didn't have the strength to explain it to him face-to-face and was glad he didn't question her. When he came around, to help with the painting or to grub out the overgrown bushes in the yard, he acted as if nothing had changed.

His behavior made her suspect that maybe their relationship hadn't meant as much to him as it had to her. He'd never promised her anything, had never said he loved her. Rachel had told her not to pin any hopes on him.

Still, it was painful. More than anything she wanted him back in her life, but she knew she couldn't let him become too important to her. So she carefully cultivated the distance she'd established. It would only make things easier when the time came. That old saying about how it was better to have loved and lost than never to have loved at all wasn't true. She didn't want to know what she would be missing when Clay left for good.

Imagining was painful enough.

Chapter Eight

Clay dialed the clinic and was surprised when Molly answered the phone.

"Well, at least you'll have to tell me yourself how busy you are, Doc. No more, like, pushing the dirty work off on, like, poor Heather." Molly had hired the teenager to work part-time in the clinic office, and he'd spoken to her often enough in the past couple of weeks to mimic her voice.

"We close at noon on Tuesdays, remember? Everyone else has gone home." Molly wanted to tell him she was all alone, and if he wanted to hurry over and take advantage of the situation, there was nothing she could do about it.

"Everyone but Super Doc," Clay said.

"Actually, I was just about to lock up. Rachel and Joe are waiting to take me to Jacksonville for lunch and to shop for things I need for the house." Molly measured her words carefully, so that Clay would not realize how glad she was to hear his voice.

"You mean you're giving us all the night off?" he asked with mock incredulity. For the past couple of weeks, family and friends alike had been drafted to get Molly's house ready. He'd stopped by as often as he could to volunteer, more than willing to be a part of the slave-labor force if that was what it took to see Molly. He'd known for some time that she was trying to avoid him, but his pride had kept him from confronting her about it. If she wanted to cool things between them, he had to respect her wishes. He didn't have to like it.

"Just about everything's been sanded, papered, painted, repaired or replaced. It's almost finished."

"So my services are no longer required," he said flatly, wishing he'd been included in her plans for the day.

"I didn't mean it like that," she apologized. "I appreciate everything you've done to help. You should go out, have some fun."

"Like a date?"

"Yes," she replied hesitantly.

"With you?"

"With someone you want to spend time with," she hedged. "I'm sure there's a long line of females who'd be interested." That was what bothered her so much. She didn't like the idea of Clay with another woman but knew she had no right to feel the way she did.

He was silent for a long moment. So she was giving him permission to go out with someone else? Obviously her recent reticence had nothing to do with her busy schedule. How could he have misread her sig nals so completely? He'd wrongly assumed that they had started to mean something to each other. Now it looked as if she wanted to give him the brush-off.

"Right." He strived for a light tone to hide his disappointment. "Give old Clay the evening off while you pursue other delights. I'll bet if your plans included cleaning the bathroom grout or replacing the septic tank, I'd have received a gilt-edged invitation."

Molly realized he was only half teasing. Before she could stop herself she added, "We'll be back by the time you close up the drugstore."

It sounded like a hint, and Clay jumped at the chance to spend some time with her. Obviously he had no pride left. "Great. We'll go to the movie and I'll buy you some popcorn."

"There's only one movie in town and we saw it last week. We took Mom and Ernie, remember?" He'd pressed her until she'd accepted, but she'd made sure they had chaperons.

"Yeah, I know. But it'll be different this time."

"How so?"

"This time we'll go alone, sit in the back row and smooch." If that didn't tell her how much he missed her, nothing would.

Molly smiled with pleasure at the image that popped into her mind. But she couldn't let the fantasy become reality. She would never be able to reconcile the incongruity of Old Doc Molly with Captain Adventure, but that didn't change the fact that she had fallen for Clay in a big way. Although it was nearly impossible when he turned on the charm, she had to follow her head, not her heart.

"I don't smooch in movies."

"You should try it sometime. We can always stop if you don't like it."

Not like it? What a silly notion. Clay's arms felt like home and the sound of his voice made her ache with need. It was much too tempting to think about.

"Sorry," she said, keeping her tone light, "but I can't make it tonight. Miss Watkins and some other ladies volunteered to come over after supper to put up the last of the wallpaper in the kitchen, and I need to finish painting the upstairs bathroom."

"I shouldn't let you know how much my ego has suffered at your hands." He sighed dramatically. "But I'm so easy when it comes to you. I'll come over and tell you all about it while we paint."

"Not that I don't appreciate it, Clay, I do. But you don't have to give up all your spare time for me. I'm sure you have more important things to do."

His grip on the phone tightened. Why did he keep subjecting himself to rejection? Hell, in the past if a woman had expected him to help her with any kind of domestic chores, he would have laid skidmarks making his exit. Now his feelings were hurt because she'd rather paint a bathroom than spend time with him.

"What color are you painting the bathroom?" he persisted.

"Why?"

"For a smart lady, you sure ask dumb questions," he joked. "So I'll know what kind of wine to bring."

"You're crazy, Cusak." She laughed, despite the little knot of doubt in her stomach.

"Okay, if you refuse to tell me, I'll just bring a white zinfandel. That goes with anything."

* * *

"If walls could talk, Doc Cooley's upstairs bathroom would have to admit it'd never contained this much excitement." Clay stood on the closed lid of the toilet. He dipped the roller into the paint tray and vigorously applied it to the wall.

"Be careful." Molly was seated on the floor, painting behind the toilet where he stood. She glanced up at him and scolded, "That's the second time you've dripped paint in my hair."

"Sorry." He rested the roller in the tray. Taking a rag from his pocket, he jumped to the floor, knelt beside her and dabbed at the hunter-green splatters. He only made the situation worse.

"You look good in this color," he told her. "You should wear it more often."

She dropped her brush and got to her feet. Leaning over the vanity, she stared with horror at the green streaks in her hair.

Clay appeared in the mirror behind her. "Just look what you've done," she accused.

He braced himself against the vanity with a hand on each side of her and leaned over to inspect the damage. His elbows threatened to give way when his thighs brushed the back of her legs and his chest touched her back. His voice was quiet when he said, "It really brings out the green in your eyes, doesn't it?"

His intense gaze in the mirror held Molly's, and she forgot all about the mess he'd made of her hair. She leaned her head backward until it rested on his shoulder.

"So you find green hair flattering on a woman?"

He hesitated only a moment before wrapping his arms around her waist, pulling her to him until their bodies were flush. His lips touched her hair. "It's very sexy. And so are you. God, Molly, I've missed you."

Before she could respond by either word or deed, Miss Watkins's voice floated up the stairs. "Yoo-hoo, Molly!"

Her heart beating wildly, Molly jerked away from him. She took a deep breath, but her answering "yes" was a bit shaky just the same.

"We're all through down here," Miss Watkins called. "How are you two getting along up there?"

Molly heard muffled giggles in the background and knew that she and Clay were the subject of the ladies' speculation. "We're nearly finished."

"No, we aren't," Clay whispered. "Not by a long shot." When he grinned, he looked just like the ornery child who'd taunted her long ago. When he lunged for her, she laughed and raced out of the room and quickly down the stairs. But he was a man now, and she knew when to make her escape.

By nine o'clock, the wallpaper had been duly admired and Clay had left to drive the four ladies home. Molly finished the painting within five minutes of their departure. She gathered up the brushes and rollers and took them downstairs to the garage to clean them.

It was a bright moonlit night, and since the double door was open, she didn't turn on the light. No point alerting the mosquitoes that dinner had arrived. She had just dropped the brushes into the soapy pail of water when the sudden onslaught of headlights blinded her.

Her hunch that it was Clay was confirmed when he pulled his car right into the garage beside her. He killed the engine and got out, holding up the bottle of wine.

"Did you forget something?" she asked, drying her hands as she walked toward him.

As soon as she was within touching distance, Clay wrapped his free arm around her waist and pulled her to him.

"Only one thing," he said suggestively.

As his lips touched hers, Molly forgot all about trying to keep her distance and allowed herself to melt against him for a brief spellbinding kiss. She'd experienced passion before, but she'd never felt a physical pull so intense and never had a man entranced her so with such a simple little kiss.

The moment their lips met, Clay became marginally aware that this was no ordinary kiss. A shiver skated along his spine when he acknowledged how much he wanted and needed Molly. The distant voice of reason told him to put an end to the madness before he was inescapably tangled in the magic.

When he finally drew back, he held Molly for several moments while he tried to make sense of his conflicting feelings. It didn't take a genius to know she wasn't the kind of woman he could discount easily. He could not have a brief passionate interlude with her and then let her go as he went on his merry bachelor way.

She was different. Dangerously different at this point in his life. She kindled feelings in him that could threaten his future plans. He had his life mapped out, and he was getting closer to his goal with each passing day. But lately, when he looked into Molly's eyes, he felt he'd reached some mystical fork in the road.

In one direction lay his well-organized plan. In the other, Molly. Good God, if he wasn't careful, she'd have him doing or saying something very stupid.

Maybe in ten years, after he'd gotten the idea of the sea out of his system, he wouldn't mind so much. But not now. The timing was all wrong. It was too soon to give into this physical thing between them. But maybe someday...

"I'd better get out of here," Clay said abruptly.

Molly stared up him, hoping her face didn't reveal the defeat she experienced at his words. Their meaning went far beyond this evening. She suspected he sensed the same inevitable ending of their relationship that she did. So she kept silent, fearing that if she spoke it would be to beg him to stay. Tonight. And forever.

"I just remembered I promised to deliver a prescription to Hattie Benson's mother." It was true, but Clay didn't mention that he'd kept that promise earlier in the evening.

She finally managed to speak around the lump in her throat. "Then you'd better go."

He stepped back and the forgotten bottle he still held clinked against his car door. He thrust the wine into her hand. "You hang on to this. Maybe we'll drink it some other time."

"Maybe." But Molly didn't think they would. She stood in the middle of her garage and stared down the street long after the car had disappeared around the corner. He was gone now and she was glad, she told herself. She really was.

* * *

When Clay pulled into his parking space at his small apartment complex, he was still trying to rationalize feelings that were totally alien to him. He had a sneaking suspicion that sometime in the past month, something important had happened, and he didn't like it at all. He was impatient with himself for even thinking about getting something started with Molly.

He'd known it was a mistake from the beginning. She wasn't the kind of woman a man could walk away from without leaving something of himself behind. He was lucky he'd caught himself before it was too late.

So what if he'd reached some stupid fork in the road? He knew which path he had to choose in the end. He'd always known. He wouldn't change his plans now. How could he?

Clay's van was five years old and paid for. His apartment, while comfortable, was plain and cramped. He'd sacrificed many luxuries to make his dreams come true, and he wasn't about to give them up now.

To continue to see Molly just wouldn't be fair. To either of them. But what was he going to do about these longings she stirred in him? Nothing, he decided. He wasn't going to call her and he most assuredly wasn't going to see her again. It was the right thing to do.

He got out of the car and slowly walked into his empty apartment. After a quick cool shower, he gathered up dirty clothes to take to the cleaner's tomorrow. When he went through the pockets of the clothes, he found a hastily scribbled name with a Jacksonville phone number on a piece of paper.

Jana? He tried, but couldn't recall a face to go with the name. He thought of Molly and tossed it into the trash. Then he remembered how she'd told him earlier to take the evening off, to go out on a date. Maybe Jana was just what the doctor ordered to take his mind off the doctor.

Clay retrieved the scrap of paper, dialed the number and invited the woman to have dinner with him the next night. He was surprised when she agreed. He still couldn't recall where they'd met, but he artfully avoided mentioning that to her. Maybe when he saw her he'd remember.

All day Wednesday, he battled the guilt feelings by telling himself it wasn't cheating. He was not committed to Molly, and she had urged him to get a date. He'd have fun if it killed him.

For at least fourteen years of his life, he'd settled for the crumbs of Molly's attention. And negative attention at that. As a child he'd operated on the soggy potato-chip principle: a soggy potato chip was better than no potato chip at all. But he was a grown man, and soggy just wouldn't cut it anymore.

The moment Clay saw Jana, he remembered they had met at the pharmaceutical convention in Miami a couple of months before. She was very attractive and they had a lot in common. Clay's interest perked up and he felt hopeful about the date.

But as the evening wore on, and the spark he'd waited so patiently for didn't materialize, his guilt feelings returned. All he could think about was Molly. Whether she knew it or not, she had come along on the date, insinuating herself between Clay and Jana.

As he drove the woman home, he wondered how Molly had spent the evening. When he walked Jana to the door, he couldn't help wishing she were Molly.

Jana unlocked her door and turned to him. "Would you like to come in for a drink?"

"It's late and I still have to drive back to Morgan's Point." Clay was almost as surprised as Jana when the glib excuse poured out of his mouth.

"I'll make coffee, instead," she offered.

He glanced at his watch. "Thanks, but not at this hour."

"It's only nine-thirty," Jana said with a frown. "I'm going to ask you an honest question, Clay. What's happened to you since Miami?"

"What do you mean?"

"When we were at the convention, you were attracted to me. And from our brief conversations I assumed we wanted the same thing from each other. Something temporary but mutually gratifying. Was I wrong?"

The woman's bluntness went way beyond honesty. She deserved an equally honest answer. "There's someone else."

She smiled. "And you were hoping I could take your mind off her, right?"

He shrugged. "This was a mistake and I owe you an apology."

"Only if you don't give me a chance," she said softly as she wrapped her arms around his neck.

Clay stiffened. In the past her assertiveness would have flattered and pleased him, but not now. When had he changed? he wondered as he removed her arms and backed away.

"I definitely owe you an apology then," he said.

Jana shook her head. "I guess tonight was a big waste of your time."

For some reason, Clay didn't think of it that way. It hadn't been a waste at all. He'd learned something very important.

It was after ten when he dialed Lydia's number, and he was relieved when Molly answered on the first ring.

"Hello, this is Dr. Fox." She sounded professional, like she was expecting the caller to need medical attention.

"Sorry to call so late," Clay said. "But I just got home."

"I just came in myself," she said softly. She didn't tell him that she'd sat on the front porch at her new house for more than an hour hoping he would come by. "I guess Mom and Ernie gave up on me and went to bed."

"Did you finish up at the house?" he asked.

"Yes. It's ready for the carpet-and-tile people."

"Who helped you? I don't suppose you even missed me."

That was laughable. She'd spent most of the evening wondering where he was and what he was doing. But she wasn't about to admit it. "I told Joe to keep Rachel at home in case there were any stray paint fumes. Mom and Ernie came over, but I sent them home early and finished the cleaning myself."

"And I picked tonight to go into Jacksonville," he said. "I'm sorry I wasn't there to help you."

"Did you have a good time?" she asked, dreading the answer.

"No," he said honestly. "Just took care of some unfinished business."

"Good," she said relieved, then quickly added, "I mean I'm glad you finished your business." Whatever it was.

"I'd rather have spent the time with you."

"I'm glad you didn't," she said. "You'll never guess what I did."

"From your tone," he said, smiling, "it must have been something ornery."

"Very. You're a bad influence."

"Are you going to tell me?"

"Jim Boyd came over and emptied the pool today. He checked it out thoroughly and filled it up again."

"Jim Boyd is a married man with a child," Clay said in a scandalized tone. "You should be ashamed of yourself."

"He left long before I even got there. I didn't even see him, you dolt." She chuckled. "I did this all by myself."

"You went skinny-dipping, didn't you?" Clay laughed. "I don't believe it."

"It felt deliciously decadent."

"And I missed it," he said sadly.

You were there, she thought, taunting me. "You didn't miss much. I remembered I hadn't locked the door and was so worried about someone stopping by that I didn't stay in the water very long."

"You're too inhibited."

"I'm cautious," she argued. "You're just too spontaneous."

"Not anymore," he said glumly. "I think you've been a bad influence on me, too."

Molly laughed. ''Well, I'd better get to bed. My days start pretty early.''

Clay didn't want the conversation to end. Only last night, he'd made the monumental decision that it would be in both their best interests to keep away from Molly Fox. But what he should do and what he felt compelled to do were two entirely different things.

Chapter Nine

The next day was Thursday, and the flooring company was scheduled to install the new carpet and tile in Molly's house. After a full day at the clinic, she stopped to inspect the results. She'd been there less than ten minutes when Clay arrived with a paper sack in each hand.

"I thought we'd celebrate the completion of your new home," he said, holding out his packages. "I brought dinner."

Molly was happy to see him, but uneasy all the same. She'd been fairly successful in avoiding him, but what would she do if they were all alone? "Mom's expecting me at home soon."

"No, she isn't. I called her while I was waiting for the chicken." He grinned, hoping to diminish the doubt in her eyes. "She said they wouldn't wait up for you."

"I don't have any furniture," she reminded him.

"No problem, we'll have a picnic." He shoved the sacks into her arms and loped back to his car. Molly watched from the doorway as he opened the trunk, grabbed something and sauntered back to the house.

She laughed when he pulled a set of sheets out of a plastic bag and spread one over the silvery gray carpet in the living room.

"What?" he asked, puzzled by her amusement.

"What kind of man carries a set of new sheets in his car?" she asked.

"The kind who hasn't had time to do his laundry for the past thirty days. I bought these this afternoon because I made arrangements with Lillie Dunlop to clean my apartment tomorrow when she finishes Joe and Rachel's place."

Lillie had been Joe's housekeeper long before he was married, and Rachel had seen no reason to change that. Her sister had never liked housework, anyway, and Lillie's husband had a medical problem that sometimes left him unable to work, so they needed the extra income.

"Is Howard Dunlop down in his back again?" Molly asked.

Clay nodded. "His prescription expired and I couldn't give Lillie a refill on the pain medication today. I suggested she bring him to see you. Did they come in?"

"No," Molly said.

"Maybe they couldn't get an appointment."

"We were busy today, but the staff always tries to fit people in if they can."

Clay shrugged. "They live several miles out. It could be they decided against making another trip today."

He mashed the paper bag flat and set out the food on top of it. "So, don't spill anything on my sheets. I don't want her to think I'm a complete pig."

While they ate chicken and sipped wine from the paper cups Clay had brought, Molly told him how well the clinic was doing. "I went over the books this morning and I'm happy to report that we show a clear profit at the end of our first thirty days in business."

"That's wonderful. The original projection was to allow at least three months for that. So, do you feel you'll able to make a good living here?"

"Yes, but the financial reward isn't the best part," Molly said. "It's the appreciation and gratitude of the townspeople, and the way they've made a place for me. I can't imagine living anywhere else."

"It's a great place to settle down," Clay agreed. His own second thoughts about leaving Morgan's Point for good were driving him crazy. Granted, he still dreamed of sailing off into the sunset, but doing it alone no longer held quite the same appeal. He wondered if, when the time came, he could leave Molly behind? After the way she'd treated him lately, he was worried she might not even miss him when he was gone.

"Yes," she said, reminding herself that Clay wasn't ready to settle down. "I think I'll be happy here. And I love this house. Was Doc Cooley an avid swimmer?"

He shook his head. "Doc had the pool installed a couple of years ago—claimed he didn't get enough exercise. But Jim Boyd was just starting up his pool business, and he and Lou Ann were struggling. I think Doc just wanted to help them out."

Molly smiled. It would be hard to replace a man as well liked as Doc Cooley. But she was willing to try. "At the risk of repeating myself, I love this town."

Finished with the meal, they quietly gathered up the remains of the picnic and Clay took the paper bag outside to the garbage can. When he came back, Molly was sitting on the fireplace hearth with a stack of papers in her lap. Clay sat down beside her.

"What are you doing with those?" he asked.

"These are pictures of the furniture I ordered and I'm trying to decide where to place everything."

"Hmm," he said, looking at the picture of the overstuffed traditional living-room set. "I like that sofa. It looks roomy and comfortable."

Molly hadn't realized until this moment that she'd unconsciously chosen her furniture with Clay in mind. She'd thought of his long frame stretched out on the couch and selected one to accommodate him. Suddenly she was afraid to show him the rest of the pictures. It wouldn't do for him to realize that she'd planned her home around him.

"Let me see," he said taking the pictures from her. "I'm no decorator, but I think it would be nice to have the sofa facing the fireplace. Gazing into a fire can be cozy and romantic on long winter evenings."

Molly had thought the same thing when she'd ordered it. That was before she'd made her decision to keep Clay out of her life. Now she didn't like to think about the lonely nights ahead of her. She laughed nervously. "How romantic can a fake fireplace be?"

"It's all in the wrist." Clay flipped the switch and the carefully constructed lights began to give off the illusion of a well-laid fire in the hearth. He took her hand and sat down on the floor. "Romance with an electric fireplace is somewhat of a challenge. You have to create your own heat. Come down here and I'll show you what I mean."

Her hand still in his, Molly kneeled in front of him.

She turned her face and stared into the play of lights. She didn't want him to see through the lie she was about to tell.

"I don't feel a thing."

Clay came up on his knees and they were inches apart. With one finger he traced the line of her jaw and turned her face to his.

"Let me know when you feel something," he said softly.

His head lowered and their lips met. He trailed his fingers along her shoulder. The whisper-soft touch held a magic all its own, and her knees weakened, causing her to lean into him. He wrapped his arms around her and pulled her close.

He'd been right about creating heat. She felt his warmth and gave in to the impulse to melt against him. The uneven rhythm of his breathing told her of his response.

Clay was pleased by the way Molly moved against him. He deepened the kiss, wanted it to go on forever, but suddenly there was an interruption. He tore his lips away, trailing moist kisses to her earlobe.

"Someone's ringing your doorbell," he said, pointing out the obvious.

"Is that what I hear?" Molly's arms were still tightly wrapped around his waist, and forcing herself to let go, she sat back on her heels. With trembling hands, she fluffed her hair and smoothed her skirt.

Now someone pounded on the door. Clay stood and gave Molly a hand up. He chuckled. "I wasn't sure at first—my ears were already ringing. But I'm positive now. We have company."

Molly walked to the door on shaky legs and pulled it open. "Hello, boys."

Mike Hacker stood there; behind him his brother, Larry, held a bundle in his arms. "Dr. Fox, we're sorry to bother you, but we've got a problem. We were kind of hoping you might help us."

"I'll do what I can. Why don't you come inside and tell me about it."

Mike gestured at the bundle. "We'd better stay out here. We found a sick cat and Uncle Wayne's out on patrol. Would you drive us to the Taylor place?"

"Of course," Molly said. She was relieved that this particular medical emergency was out of her jurisdiction. The Taylors were veterinarians who ran an animal hospital next door to their home a few miles outside town.

Clay followed her to the door. "I'll come with you."

"Good, you can drive. I'm acquainted with Bill and Madison—they brought Davey and little Sara to the clinic for their booster shots. But I'm not sure I can find their place in the dark."

Later, Bill Taylor answered the door and invited them into the house. He took one look at the pathetic-looking cat and whisked it away to the clinic promising to examine it and get back to them as soon as he could. Madison served lemonade and cookies to the unexpected guests.

Their small son, Davey, raced into his bedroom and came back with an armload of miniature action heroes, which he proudly displayed for Mike and Larry. Sara pulled herself up to the coffee table and took a tentative step toward the couch. She promptly fell on her bottom, but gamely tried again.

"Does the cat belong to you, Molly?" Madison asked.

"No, Mike and Larry found it," she explained. "Clay and I just gave them a ride out here."

"Officer Hacker was out on patrol," Clay added.

"Well, I'm not glad an animal is sick," Madison said, "but I am glad you're here. I tried to call you both this evening to invite you over for burgers Saturday night. Rachel and Joe are coming, and after we put the children to bed, we can play cards and talk."

"Sounds great." Clay didn't bother to consult Molly. Remembering, he turned to her and added, "We'd talked about taking in a movie, but we can do that anytime. Right, Doc?"

"Sure." Molly managed to smile brightly in spite of her hesitation. It appeared that Bill and Madison, as well as other people, already considered her and Clay a couple. Not only would she suffer a broken heart when he left, but everyone in town would know about it.

Bill came into the room alone. "The cat'll be all right, but she's suffering from malnutrition. I put her on an IV and I want to keep her for a day or two to make sure she doesn't have any other problems. Once she gets her shots, I can give her a clean bill of health."

"Thanks, Dr. Taylor," Mike said.

"I'll give you boys a call tomorrow and let you know when you can come and get her."

The brothers exchanged glances, and Mike was elected spokesman again. "We can't keep her because she might not get along with Uncle Wayne's drug dog. She strayed into the yard this afternoon and looked so sick we didn't know what else to do but bring her here."

"Yeah," Larry agreed. "We were hoping you could find her a home."

Molly spoke up. "I should be moved into my house by Sunday—I could take her. I haven't had a cat since I was a kid."

"I remember LuLu the attack cat," Clay said with a laugh. "She hated me with a passion."

"You never should have sprayed her with the garden hose," Molly told him. "LuLu was a sweetie. She just had a thing about baths."

"She was stalking me," Clay retorted. "The hose was my only means of self-defense. I was only five."

Madison and Bill laughed. "I didn't realize you two went so far back," he said.

"Way back." Clay smiled at Molly and the warmth of his memories softened his expression. Somewhere along the way, he'd almost forgotten what an important role she'd played in his past. She'd been a part of his life for a long time, and the twelve years they'd been apart seemed insignificant compared to those they'd spent together. The thought of losing her again was frightening.

After leaving the Taylor place, Clay dropped off the boys, then drove Molly back to her house to pick up her car. Surprised when she quickly opened the door and jumped out, he leaned across the passenger seat. "Molly?"

She turned around, bent over at the waist and rested one hand on the door. "What?"

"I had grandiose plans of picking up where we left off." He put his hand over hers, longing to share what was in his heart, but unable to find the words. "Want to come over to my apartment for a cup of coffee?"

"I have a busy day tomorrow." Molly withdrew her hand from his. If he continued to touch her, she might not find the resolve to resist him. "Besides, I'm not sure I want to venture into the home of a man who hasn't done laundry in a month. Funny, but you don't smell like a man who hasn't done his housework."

Clay's laugh was forced. He knew she was avoiding him again and cursed the interruption that had taken her from his arms. "Thanks to Pearl's Dry Clean and Laundry. But I'll have you know I make my bed and do the dishes every morning. As the child of a working mother, I learned early in life to hang up my clothes and pick up after myself. Not all men are slobs, you know."

"Then you're not a typical bachelor?" she teased.

"No, I'm not." If she'd asked him that a few weeks ago his answer would have been a resounding yes. But not now. The typical bachelor didn't contemplate changing his plans for the future to accommodate a woman. He opened the passenger door. "Get in here, Molly."

"Why?"

"So, I can kiss you good-night without an audience."

Molly got inside. There were no more words exchanged and his embrace was quick and welcome. Their lips met and she no longer cared about the audience or anything else. She didn't resist when Clay pulled her onto his lap.

After long moments, his lips slipped from hers to follow a path down her face, her neck, her shoulders. His arms tightened around her, and Molly delighted in the tension of his muscles. One of his hands found its way under her blouse, languidly rubbing her back. Reason was no longer a viable option.

"You folks oughtta get married," said a voice at the window. "Then you'd have a home to go to."

Molly gasped when she saw Officer Hacker's grin. She buried her face in Clay's neck, more embarrassed than she'd ever been in her life.

"We're not breaking any laws, are we, Wayne?" Clay smiled into the bright beam of the flashlight the police officer directed their way.

"Well, your car *is* pointed in the wrong direction to be parked on this side of the street," the lawman pointed out. "But I won't give you a ticket. With your hands being so full and all, I don't see how you could get to your wallet for your license, anyhow. And since you're just dropping the lady off, I'll let it slide this time."

"I appreciate that. Now, would you mind turning that thing off?" Clay asked pleasantly.

"Sure thing," Officer Hacker said. He flicked the button and blessed darkness returned. "You two move on now. We can't have you settin' a bad example for the teenagers." Slapping one end of the flashlight against his palm, he turned on his heel and walked back to his patrol car. He pulled alongside them and rolled down his window.

"But if you're planning to be a while, you might want to turn the car around. Good night, Clay."

"Good night. And thanks," Clay called as he drove away. "For nothing," he added under his breath.

Molly laughed as she wriggled out of his arms. "How humiliating to be caught necking in the dark at our age."

"Yeah, we should know better. Hey, where are you going?" he asked as she scooted from his lap and into the other seat.

"Home. Before he comes back." She opened the door and got out again. "The weekly paper is due out tomorrow and I fully expect to see the whole sordid story in two-inch headlines."

"Hope they spell our names right," he teased. "Just think of it as free advertising. Call me tomorrow when you have some free time?"

"All right," she said, not knowing if she would or not. Common sense had a tendency to return with the sunlight. "Good night, Clay."

"Good night," he replied. As he watched Molly drive away, he couldn't help wondering if there were forces at work trying to keep them apart.

The next afternoon, Clay received a surprise call from his investment counselor. He listened in quiet amazement as she explained how his speculations had paid off in big round numbers. He'd agreed to the long shots she'd recommended because he trusted her judgment and because he enjoyed the inherent challenge of taking risks. He'd never expected such immediate and mind-boggling returns.

By the time he hung up the phone, he knew that his someday was now. His five-year plan had been miraculously shortened into less than two. The dream didn't have to be a dream anymore. He could now afford the reality. If any event ever called for a celebration, this one did.

He called a semiretired pharmacist who sometimes substituted for him and asked if he'd like to finish out the day for him. As soon as he could slip away, Clay stopped by his apartment to change and pack a cooler, then took off for Lake Sampson and the solitude needed to process the information he'd just received.

Before long, he was deftly guiding the sailboat out to the middle of the lake. When he found a spot to his liking, he lowered the sails. Stripping down to his swimsuit, he opened the cooler. In the future he'd keep a bottle of champagne on hand for such occasions, but for now a light beer would have to do. He popped the top and gestured toward the sun with the can.

"I did it!" It was as much question as it was statement. He still couldn't believe the insanity of his good luck. Molly had once asked him if everything he touched turned to gold, and now he had to wonder at his good fortune. No one should get everything they want so easily.

He took a long cooling drink of beer. The day was hot and the beer slid down his throat with comforting ease. He finished it off, put the empty back in the cooler and pulled out another. He inserted a compact disc into the portable player and settled back against the deck cushions, allowing the rhythmic tunes of classic rock to wash over him while the boat undulated gently on the water.

"Molly would have enjoyed this," he said to no one. It was peaceful on the lake at this time of day during the week. Very soothing, almost romantic, he decided as he listened to the sound of the water slapping softly against the hull. If he'd waited a couple of hours, maybe she would have been free to come along and help him celebrate.

"Molly." Clay sighed, closed his eyes and placed the cold can against his forehead. Celebrating alone wasn't as much fun as it used to be.

After his third beer, he toasted the water. "You've been a great substitute for the ocean, Lake Sampson, but I don't have to settle for your limited boundaries anymore."

He popped another top. "I can afford to buy a boat that'll make this one look like a bathtub toy. And I don't have to wait. I can leave Morgan's Point anytime I choose!"

Or could he?

"Damn," he swore, and took another drink. If he was about to have everything he'd ever wanted, why did the celebration feel so empty? Why did the prospect of leaving Morgan's Point seem so bleak?

There was a one-word answer to all his questions. Molly.

For the past two years he'd been working single-mindedly toward this goal. Now that it was time to realize it, he was filled with doubt. Not about his feelings for Molly, though; those had always remained constant, he realized, for more than twenty years.

Somewhere along the way his dream had changed without his realizing it. It included Molly now, whether she liked the idea or not. Even if he could persuade her to go away with him, which he seriously doubted, a boat was no place to raise children. Children? Where had that thought come from? Confirmed bachelors didn't include children in their plans, did they?

So maybe he wasn't cut out to be a bachelor, after all. Or a sailor, for that matter. What if he never ventured farther than Lake Sampson's boundaries? It was a very nice lake.

As Clay sat in the sun, the boat rocking gently beneath him, he realized that he wanted Molly Fox at any cost. There was a reason he'd never shared his celebrations with a woman. The women weren't Molly. When self-awareness came, it came strong. Just like some people keep a guest room tidy and ready for company, Clay had always kept a part of his heart ready for Molly. He'd never gotten seriously involved with other women because there was no one else but her.

During his vulnerable years, when he could have easily fallen in love, he'd convinced himself that he loved Rachel. But now he knew why he never really had. Fancying himself in love with Rachel was safe, for she would never return his feelings. But carrying that imagined torch had enabled him to remain on the fringes of Molly's life. He'd kept up with her through Lydia and Rachel. He hadn't acknowledged it then, but he'd been stricken with fear whenever her family reported a man in her life.

He'd loved her since he was kid and he'd love her when he was a toothless old man. God! Why had he never told her? He set sail for the marina and a phone. He had to find out if Molly would have him before he made further plans. She didn't know it yet, but today was a momentous occasion.

Clay dialed the clinic number and asked to speak to Molly. He had a short wait before he heard her welcome voice.

"Dr. Fox," she answered.

"Hi," he said. "It's Clay."

"Hello, Clay."

"Molly, let's have dinner tonight. We need to talk."

"My goodness, you sound awfully serious."

"Who, me? Serious?" he said, evading the issue. He wouldn't reveal his thoughts over the telephone. If he was going to propose, he wanted candlelight and roses. A man who intended to sweep a woman right off her feet needed the works.

Chapter Ten

Molly agreed to see Clay, but by the time she hung up the phone she was having second thoughts. He had told her to wear something fancy, that they were going to a special place.

Their relationship had been teetering on the brink of an affair for weeks. Was he growing as frustrated with the situation as she? Should she throw caution to the wind, knowing he couldn't make the commitment she wanted?

One day in the future, Clay was going to sail away and leave her landlocked and lonely. He had his own personal agenda, which did not include offering her the permanency she needed.

Except for that small flaw, he was perfect. He was considerate and thoughtful, fun to be with, and he drove her crazy with desire. That was the problem.

When he touched her, kissed her, the differences between them did not seem insurmountable.

She'd often heard, but never quite believed, that with love, all things were possible. With love, compromises could be made, bargains struck. Right now she wanted badly to believe that. Her only fear was that she cared too much, needed too much. But when she thought about a future without him, she promised herself she would be satisfied with what he was willing to give. She fervently hoped it would be enough.

Eager to see him, she left the clinic as soon as possible and stopped at Rachel's to borrow something to wear. Then she rushed to her mother's house and took a quick shower. As she zipped herself into the little black dress Rachel had deemed perfect for such an occasion, she kept looking out the window for Clay.

Impulsiveness had an invigorating effect on her spirit, and when she heard his van pull into her mother's driveway, she raced to the door and threw it open. A wave of doubt washed over her, and she slowed, took a deep breath and walked out onto the porch to meet him.

She forgot all about her doubts when Clay bounded up the steps toward her. Looking happier than she'd seen him look in a long time, he gave her a lingering hug. She cupped his face in her hands to memorize the joy there and surrendered to a kiss that didn't last nearly long enough.

"Hi," she said breathlessly when she could bear to end it. "I'm ready."

"Hi, yourself." He wrapped her more tightly in his arms. "You look beautiful."

Molly backed away, conscious of the neighbors who had come outside to watch. "You look like you got some sun today."

"I went out on the boat this afternoon," he explained as he helped her into the van. He kissed her nose before closing the door.

She watched him walk around the car, and doubt returned with sickening force. Why couldn't she make a decision about Clay and stick with it? What did she want? She wanted to hold on to him and never let go. She wanted to wake up each morning wrapped in his arms, then send him off to work with plans to meet for lunch. She wanted to argue with him about the things married people argued about, wanted to bear his children. She wanted to grow old with him in Morgan's Point and play bridge at the seniors center.

Was that too much to ask?

Or was it too little? Maybe it wasn't fair to ask Clay to settle for such routine pleasures when he had his heart set on the sea. Reason kicked in and she realized she was headed for disaster if she didn't cool things between them before it was too late.

The restaurant where Clay took her was on the highway midway between Morgan's Point and Sinola. It didn't cater to tourists or families on their way to Disney World. The decor was that of understated elegance, the romantic ambience obvious, but not strained. The lighting was indirect, and candles and flowers gave the tables a personal touch. A pretty woman dressed in a sultry sequined gown sang at the piano bar. It was precisely the kind of intimate place she had dreamed about going to with Clay. And the kind she feared the most.

The hostess ushered them to a quiet alcove. Molly scooted across the banquette, and as Clay slid in beside her, a waiter appeared with the menu. Clay ordered a bottle of champagne.

Molly glanced at him. "Are we celebrating?"

"Oh, yeah. You're the first woman I've ever wanted to share a celebration with."

The unexpected confession unsettled him. Please, Lord, he prayed, don't let me botch this. Molly really did look beautiful tonight. Her shiny hair was loose and tempting, her dress revealing in its simplicity. But it wasn't the softly rounded curves, the creamy skin or the pretty face that attracted him to her.

Why did she make him want things he'd never wanted before? Why did everything take on more meaning when they were together? And why was he worrying about it now?

She smiled at the waiter as he poured their champagne. "You certainly are in a rare mood. I haven't heard one joke out of you tonight, Clay."

"I guess I'm a little nervous. I don't know where to start." When the waiter left he said, "I've got this woman on my mind and I can't stop thinking about her. Most of all I don't want to stop."

She gazed into his eyes and saw her reflection there. His intensity disturbed her.

"You make me forget there are other women in the world, Molly."

"I feel that way around you, too," she admitted. "And I've learned something from you about how to live for the moment." She had to say it before she lost her nerve. "That's what I've decided to do."

"That's another thing I love about you—you never fail to surprise me."

Another thing he loved about her! Molly held those words close to her heart and clung to them.

"I have some good news to share with you," he said. But before he could tell her, the waiter was back to ask if they were ready to order.

"Not yet," Clay told him curtly. "We'll let you know."

"What's wrong?" she asked. It wasn't like Clay to be sharp with anyone.

"My investment counselor called today."

"That's the good news?"

"To make an amazing long story short, I'm suddenly a wealthy man." He smiled. "And I've decided—"

"That's great news," Molly interrupted him with false gaiety, surprised that she didn't choke on the lie. With a sinking feeling, she realized exactly what she'd let herself in for when she'd fallen in love. "Now you'll be able to buy the boat you want and move up the date of your departure."

Clay studied her intently. He was hurt that she could let him go so easily. "And that doesn't bother you?"

Bother her? It was killing her. Molly picked up her glass and feigned a happiness she did not feel. She wouldn't spoil this moment for Clay. He'd anticipated it for too long. "Let's toast your success."

Clay frowned. This was not turning out the way he'd imagined. Reluctantly he picked up his glass, clinked it against hers and took a sip.

Molly took a long gulp, hoping to dislodge the lump in her throat. "So, when are you leaving?"

"You sound eager to get rid of me," he said with a nervous chuckle. He'd imagined several possible scenarios tonight. He'd propose and she'd accept. He'd chicken out and not propose at all. She'd have to read his mind and propose to him.

But never had he considered that she might not even care if he left. Might even be glad to see him go. Suddenly he felt like an awkward teenager. The unworthy kid who had to steel himself against ultimate rejection from the beautiful creature who considered him a pest.

"Of course I'm not," Molly said truthfully. "But I know it's what you want. What you've been working for."

"Not since you came here," he said cautiously.

Molly stared into his blue eyes, finding the flame of the candle reflected in twin columns of fire. His gaze, as intimate as a caress, was sincere. "That's very flattering, Clay. But unnecessary."

"It wasn't meant to be flattering. I don't want to leave you, Molly."

"That's sweet, Clay, but be realistic." Molly wasn't sure where she found the strength to go on. "We want different things out of life, so there's really no reason for you to change your plans. Go. Do what you've always wanted to do."

His gaze was more intense than ever. "All I need, all I want, is you. Nothing else matters."

Molly fought the tears that welled in her eyes. Pain and wanting fought in her heart. "Maybe it's a good thing we don't always get what we want."

His voice was accusing and hurt. "You don't want to be with me."

"Yes, I do." The words came out in an anguished whisper. She wanted to plead with him to stay, but she knew she had to do this for both their sakes. Otherwise, there might come a day when they would both regret it.

"There's something wonderful between us," he said, taking her hand in his. "I'm just beginning to understand it and I've always been in awe of it. I've made up my mind. I'm staying."

"For how long?"

Clay frowned, unsure what she was asking.

She misunderstood his hesitation and yanked her hands from his, summoning anger to help her deal with regret. "I admit we were on the verge of something. Maybe just an affair, maybe more. But it's probably a good thing that nothing happened."

"I don't know about that," he argued.

"Of course it is. It'll just be over sooner this way. And you won't have to worry about leaving too soon or staying too long. No hurt feelings. No recriminations."

He raised his eyes toward the ceiling in an effort to control his own anger. But it was useless. "I want us to have more time together."

She sighed and averted her eyes. "You want! What about what *I* want?"

Clay didn't have a response for that. Molly had her practice, her family and a new home. God, she even had a cat! Maybe she didn't need him to make her happy. "Hell, your life is so full you probably won't even miss me."

"I wouldn't say that," Molly said evasively, refusing to admit how devastating the thought of his leaving really was. "Have you made up your mind when you're going?"

"I haven't even made up my mind to go. Dammit, Molly, how plain to I have to make this? How much do I have to grovel? I don't want a boat. I don't want to go to the Keys. I don't want to leave you."

"But you have to," she protested vehemently. Holding back the love she felt for him was as painful as cutting off a limb, but somehow she managed to think of all the right words. She didn't want him to sacrifice anything for her.

"Don't you see, Clay? If you don't go now, you'll be giving up a dream that's been very important to you. You'd just be settling for something else. If you let convention stand in your way, you'll always regret it."

"Why won't you listen to me?" A swift shadow of fury fell over his features and he waved his arm.

The waiter mistakenly took the gesture as his signal and returned to their table. "Are you folks ready to order?"

"No." Clay shook his head. "Something came up. We're leaving. May I have the check, please?" Without looking at it, he stood up, peeled several bills from his money clip and dropped them on the table.

Molly followed him silently from the restaurant. The ride home seemed to take forever, and she almost weakened a couple of times. She wanted to throw herself into his arms and beg him to stay, to confess that everything she'd said had been a lie. She wasn't magnanimous and generous. She was selfish and prized her own happiness above all else.

But she didn't. She loved Clay too much to deprive him of something he'd worked so hard and waited so long for. In her heart, she knew she was doing the right thing. He needed to go and get the wanderlust out of his soul once and for all. Then maybe he'd be ready to settle down for good.

To keep from crying and to lighten the tension inside the car, she said, "I get to pick up Winkum tomorrow."

"Winkum?" he asked.

"My new cat," she explained. "I went out to the Taylors to visit her during lunchtime today. She's so cute. She kept winking at me, so I named her Winkum."

He nodded glumly. Winkum. Molly's chosen companion.

"I got an important phone call today, too. My furniture is being delivered early tomorrow, so I'll be moving into my house in the morning." She knew she was jabbering but she had to keep talking. The silence begged reason.

"Will you be finished in time to make our date tomorrow night?"

"Date?" she cried incredulously.

"We were supposed to go to the Taylors for a cookout. Remember?"

"I can't do it, Clay. I'm sorry." She couldn't possibly spend the evening with him. It was time the world stopped thinking of her and Clay as a couple. "It's going to be a long hard day tomorrow, and with Winkum fresh out of the vet hospital, I don't see how I could go off and leave her."

He pulled into her mother's driveway, slammed on the brakes and killed the engine. "Looks like I've already been replaced." Clay slapped the steering wheel with his palm. "And by a damn cat!"

"That's unreasonable and you know it," she said hotly. She opened the passenger door, jumped out and slammed it behind her for emphasis.

Clay slammed his door, too, and raced her to the porch. He got there first and threw himself in front of the door, blocking her escape. "I'm the one being dumped," he said, thumping his chest. "I'm the one who has a right to be angry."

"You're not being dumped," she denied. "I'm just trying to make it easier for you to go after what you want."

Clay rolled his eyes heavenward. "You need to have your hearing checked, Doc. I don't want to go!"

"But you said—"

"There's something I haven't said." His eyes searched hers for encouragement. Finding none, he put his hands on her hips and said it, anyway. "I love you, Molly. I want to marry you."

"You're just making this more difficult." She shook her head, fighting desperately to hold back the threatening tears. But there was nothing she could do about the raw grief that gnawed at her heart. Her voice was dispirited when she added, "Don't do this, Clay. Not now."

"If not now, when?" he asked, his lips too close for comfort.

"I don't know," she said breathlessly.

He pulled her roughly into his arms and his eyes pleaded with her. His voice was thick and unsteady. "I have to kiss you."

His lips sought hers, claiming them in a most proprietary manner. His tongue moved like a fiery brand inside her mouth, tasting, savoring. She melted into his embrace, her breasts crushed against his chest.

His hands swept down the sides of her body, over the tight material of her dress. Then they moved slowly over her hips, her waist, and upward to her breasts.

She hugged him fiercely for a moment, then pushed him away before she was totally lost. "Go on, Captain Adventure. Experience freedom. When you've had enough, come back."

Confused anger swept across the beloved features of his face. He stomped around the porch. "Nothing is going to change your mind, is it?"

"Don't shout at me," she yelled, hot tears running freely down her cheeks. "And no, I won't change my mind. This is something you have to do for both our sakes. You have a right to your dream. I don't want to worry for the rest of my life that you'll regret giving it up for me."

"That's ridiculous!" he yelled.

"That's how I feel. I love you too much to let you come to resent me later."

"You love me?" His anger turned into a grin. "You really love me." Clay gently took her in his arms again and rubbed her back soothingly. "I'm sorry I yelled at you. I never want to make you cry, Molly."

"Clay." She sighed as he lowered his head.

He watched her eyes flutter shut and her lips part in anticipation. He gently kissed one temple, then the other, then the delicate curve of an eyebrow. Without haste, he tasted her, enjoying the soft texture of her skin. Her lips beckoned, but he nibbled along the line of her jaw and the hollow of her cheek.

Molly felt his thumb stroke her bottom lip as he whispered kisses over her face. Her breath escaped in a soft sigh as he sipped at the corners of her mouth. He brushed lightly over her lips, retreating when she would have sought more pressure. With a moan she slipped her fingers into his hair and pulled his lips to hers. It was a goodbye kiss, filled with longing and desperation. She ended it abruptly.

"Go, Clay."

"Why do you always try to send—"

Molly placed a trembling finger over his lips to stop the tortured words. "Please," she begged. "Go."

"I'm going," he said finally, and his voice held a warning tone. "But I'll be back."

Chapter Eleven

Molly stepped into her mother's house and closed the door softly behind her. She listened, but it was several minutes before Clay started his engine and drove away. She leaned against the door until the sound of his van was lost to the night.

The silence welled up around her and she slid to the floor. Now she knew what sorrow meant. Exhausted by indecision, she wept until her heart was empty. Empty of tears and emotion, but never empty of love for Clay.

Making it through the day Saturday was like an obstacle course. Getting up and dressing took an incredible amount of willpower, and she felt drained by the effort. Moving into her new home seemed an impossible feat.

On the other hand, Rachel and Lydia were cheerful and full of energy. Once the furniture was in place,

Lydia sent Ernie and Joe out to pick up Winkum just to get them out from underfoot. She sent the girls to the kitchen to put away dishes while she tackled the linen closets.

At one point Rachel stopped arranging glasses on a shelf and turned to her sister. "Molly, what's wrong with you?"

"I'm tired," she said truthfully. "Crying most of the night takes a lot out of a person."

"Mom said your eyes were red and puffy this morning. You and Clay have a disagreement?"

"Not really."

Molly told Rachel about last night's disastrous date. Then she finished, "We agreed that he should leave Morgan's Point."

Rachel frowned. "I can't believe he still wants to go. He's been so attentive to you lately. I thought all that was going somewhere."

Lydia came into the room. "Where is Clay going?"

"You're getting pretty good at listening through keyholes, Mom." But Molly, realizing she'd have no peace until she explained, told them what had happened.

Lydia sat down at the table and put her head in her hands. Then she looked up at the ceiling. "Lord, how did I ever manage to raise two such intelligent, yet foolish daughters?"

"Now, Mom," Rachel scolded, "that's not nice. I didn't let Joe get away."

"You were the one leaving, Rachel. It was Joe who didn't let you get away," Lydia said stubbornly. "But Molly, you take the prize. You're sending Clay away."

"And he doesn't want to go," Rachel added.

"Someone needs to have a talk with that boy," Lydia said thoughtfully.

"Mom, Rachel, please listen to me." Molly sat down at the other end of the table. "I want everyone to butt out. Clay is not a boy. He's a grown man and I'm a grown woman. Right or wrong, we have to make our own decisions. He's an adventurer who got stuck in a small-town rut, but now that he has the chance, he has to go. Don't you see?"

"No!" Lydia declared. "You said he told you he wanted to stay, that he told you he loved you and even proposed." She sighed. "I'm sorry, but that just doesn't sound to me like a man who's dying to escape."

Rachel nodded. "I have to agree with Mom on this one, Molly. When this attraction began, I warned you about his inability to make a commitment. But I've noticed a change in him lately. I think I was wrong."

"Rachel—" Molly began, but Rachel interrupted her.

"Just let me finish. I've never known Clay to lie. If he said he loves you and wants to stay, then he probably does."

"Or thinks he does," Molly said despondently. "He might not regret changing his whole life for me at first. Not while our love's fresh and new. But what about later? What happens when the kids get on his nerves, the car won't start and the basement floods? The mundane can make romance seem like a bad idea. He'll always wonder what might have been."

Rachel and Lydia smiled at each other and shook their heads.

Molly glared at them. "What's the joke?"

Lydia shrugged, but Rachel was undaunted by her sister's irritability.

"When the kids get on his nerves, you can dump them on me or Mom, or hire a baby-sitter. Clay's a wealthy man, and you have money of your own. You can buy a new car or fix the old one if it won't start. And if the basement floods, you'll just have to call a plumber. People do it every day all over the world, and it hardly ever interferes with true love."

Molly bit her lip.

Rachel took her hand and squeezed it. "Those are excuses, Molly, not reasons. You're just afraid. I can understand that."

"If you love Clay," Lydia said softly, putting her hands over those of her daughters, "you'd better think about all this real hard."

"I have," Molly said. "I've thought of little else since we parted last night."

"It'll all work out the way it's supposed to." Lydia patted Molly's shoulder and rose to her feet. "Let's get busy and get this over with."

By the time Joe and Ernie returned with the cat, the move was officially complete. Joe and Rachel were due at the Taylors' at seven, so they went home to allow Rachel some rest before their evening out. Lydia and Ernie tried to coax Molly into coming home with them for dinner.

"I can't," she said. "I told the Taylors I needed to stay home tonight for Winkum's sake. I wouldn't want them to hear that I went somewhere else."

After everyone left, Molly wandered into the living room and closed the front door, leaving the windows open for the cool breeze. She sat on the sofa, which faced the mock fireplace just as Clay had suggested. She'd only moved into the house today, and already it was full of reminders of him.

Needing comfort, Molly picked up the long-haired tortoiseshell cat. Winkum submitted to several minutes of petting and cooing, but her attention span was short. The animal squirmed for freedom and Molly allowed her to leave her arms. Loving something, or someone, too much was just as bad as not loving it enough.

Winkum pranced around, inspecting and sniffing everything in sight. When she finished she sat up and looked at Molly as if something was amiss. Her left eye tweaked and Molly smiled.

Bill Taylor had told her the animal wasn't really winking, that the movement was only a reflexive tic. Perhaps due to rough treatment the cat had received in her past. But Molly believed Winkum knew exactly how adorable she was.

"Meow."

"Don't you start on me, Winkum. I know he ought to be here, and he would have been if I hadn't turned him away."

The left eye blinked again.

"So, you think I should call him, huh?" Molly asked. "Well, I'm not going to, no matter how badly I want to see him. He might think I've changed my mind."

Winkum made a noise that was a low rumble in her chest. Not exactly a purr, more of a reprimand.

"No," Molly said vehemently. "I love him too much. I couldn't bear it if his love for me turned to resentment in the years to come."

Winkum rubbed against her legs and Molly picked her up again. Full of feline sympathy, the cat didn't move a muscle while her new mistress wept all over her.

On Sunday she stayed close to the house and didn't even go to church. She even turned down a dinner invitation from her mother. She was afraid of running into Clay, worried she might throw herself into his arms and beg him to stay. The day was long and boring, and she couldn't have handled the mocking solitude if it hadn't been for Winkum. But she knew she had to get herself together so that she could go into the clinic on Monday morning as bright and alert as usual.

On Monday, Molly was eager to get to work and hoped it would take her mind off Clay. But it seemed half the population of Morgan's Point had heard the news about his windfall and dropped by to get a firsthand look at how Molly was taking the news.

She pasted a bright smile on her face and muttered dozens of platitudes about how fortunate Clay Cusak was. The playacting drained her. By the time evening came, she was exhausted and barely had the energy to feed Winkum and herself. She left the dishes in the sink to be dealt with another day.

She had just settled down on the sofa with a journal when the doorbell rang. She practiced smiling all the way to the door because she didn't want to give her unexpected visitor, whoever it might be, a hint of her inner turmoil. When she opened it, Clay stood there, frowning.

"Is something wrong?" she asked.

"No more than usual," he said. "Do I have to have a medical emergency to get invited inside?"

"Of course not. It's just that you look so fierce." Molly stepped back. "Come in, Clay."

"It shows, huh?" He closed the door behind him. "Too bad, but that's the way I'm feeling these days."

"Would you like to see the house?" she asked.

"No," he said flatly. "I can't stay. My plane leaves in an hour."

"Oh," she said as brightly as she could manage, hoping to hide the pain. "I'm glad to see you aren't wasting any time."

Clay didn't know what to do. Molly was more than willing to tell him goodbye, and his only plan of action was some misguided notion involving pulling her into his arms and kissing her until their knees turned to jelly. He stuck his hands into his pockets before they could act of their own volition.

"I'm flying to St. Augustine on business, and I wanted to let you know there will be a substitute pharmacist in the store for a few days."

"Thanks, I appreciate your coming by." Molly bent and picked up her cat, who was rubbing against Clay's legs. She hesitated before looking at him again, hoping to see his infernal grin. But when she looked up, he wasn't smiling. "This is Winkum."

"How do you do, Winkum."

Clay reached out and caressed the cat's chin. The animal went limp in her arms and purred. Molly understood, because she, too, responded in much the same way when Clay touched her.

"She likes you," she said, hugging Winkum against her breast. And I love you, she thought. And I might just change my mind about letting you go, if only you'd say again that you want to stay. Just tell me one more time.

Clay was filled with envy as he watched the cat nuzzle Molly. "Well, I'd better go." He fished in his shirt pocket and pulled out a slip of paper. "This is the number where I'll be staying if anyone should need me." Or if anyone should change her mind and realize she was throwing away a perfectly good chance for true happiness, he added silently.

Molly took the paper and put it in her pocket without looking at it. Don't go, she begged silently. "Have a good trip."

Clay nodded, opened the door and left without saying anything else. Molly locked up and went upstairs to climb into her lonely bed.

Tuesday morning, Lillie Dunlop brought her husband to the clinic. "Howard's run out of pain medication, and Clay says he can't refill it without a new prescription. I called, but your receptionist said he ought to come in and let you look him over. So here we are."

After Molly checked Howard Dunlop, she gave her diagnosis. "You have arthritis, Mr. Dunlop, probably due to a back injury from the past."

Howard snorted. "We already knew that. What we want you to do is give me a prescription to help me stand the pain enough so I can get back to work."

"I don't think that's the answer. We'd only be treating the symptom, not the problem," Molly said firmly.

"Doc Cooley said the same thing," Lillie put in. "But those other pills were expensive, and it was like taking a dose of water. We decided not to waste our money on any refills of those."

Molly hoped she'd be able to change their minds. She checked Howard's file. "I see Doc Cooley also put you on an exercise program. Have you been walking for thirty minutes each day, Howard?"

"Not with this pain," he grumbled.

"It might help. There are some wonderful new drugs now, and we're going to find one that helps you. There was a salesman here yesterday and he left me some samples. I'll get them for you if you promise to try them."

Howard frowned, but his answer was affirmative.

Molly went to her office and called the drugstore. She didn't really have any samples, but she would pay for the pills herself if that was the only way to get Mr. Dunlop to take them.

She spoke with the substitute pharmacist, ordered the prescription and sent Heather running to pick it up. During her brief conversation with the man, he unwittingly let it slip that Clay had gone to St. Augustine to buy a boat.

She hung up the phone and rested her chin in her hand. So that's why he was hurrying off. He was doing exactly what she had encouraged him to do. What really hurt was that he hadn't cared enough about her feelings to tell her he was taking her advice.

At least she knew now. It was really over. Clay was moving ahead with his precious plan. He was getting on with his life. She slapped her palm on the desk. And that was what she had to do, too. Work would take her mind off him, and she planned to bury herself in it right up to her eyebrows.

In the past, Molly had been successful in allowing the needs of her patients to override her own, and she could do it again. She swiped at her eyes, vowing not to shed another tear over what might have been.

A few minutes later, Heather skidded into the room. "Here's that prescription you ordered. Like, what does STAT mean?"

"It means I wanted it, like, fast, Heather. Thank you."

"Hey, Doc, have you been crying?"

"I had something in my eye." Molly plucked a tissue from the box on the desk and blew her nose.

"Yeah, right," Heather said. "Clay Cusak is a jerk."

"No, he isn't," Molly said softly. "He's a very nice man with some traveling to get out of his system."

"But he jilted you."

"No, he didn't. Things hadn't gotten that far."

"Well, he broke your heart, then," the girl protested loyally.

"It's not broken. It's only cracked a little. I did that, Heather, by allowing myself to want too much." Molly shrugged and tried hard to believe her next words. "Clay and I have been friends a long time. We'll always be friends."

"Friends!" Heather looked at Molly with imagined teenage experience. "Yeah, right, Doc. Whatever you say."

Molly put the prescription into the pocket of her lab coat and began formulating her story for the Dunlops. Then, taking a deep breath, she squared her shoulders and strode toward the examining room. It was time to get back to doing what she did best, to what it seemed she was destined to do.

Taking care of other people's problems.

Chapter Twelve

Clay hadn't been altogether honest with Molly when he'd told her he was going to St. Augustine. Had she known just what his business there entailed, she might have felt honor-bound to try to talk him out of it.

He'd suffered greatly while he was away and was eager to get home and put his new revised plan into action. Since news traveled fast in Morgan's Point, Joe was the only person who knew about it, and he'd been sworn to secrecy. He dialed Joe at his law office to tell him he was on his way home.

"How's Molly?" Clay wanted to know.

"She kept to herself last week, refusing invitations and phone calls. But after she heard you'd gone to St. Augustine to buy a boat—"

"Damn," Clay swore. "Why did you tell her that?"

"Hey, it wasn't me," Joe said defensively. "As near

as I can tell, the news was leaked by your substitute at the drugstore.''

Clay swore again. "What happened after that?"

"Molly told Rachel she was through mourning for something that couldn't be, that it was time she got on with her life the way you had. She's been spending a lot of time at the clinic, and Rachel swears she's been driving around the countryside looking for sick people to keep her busy. Personally, I don't think it's gotten quite to that point yet."

"I can't believe Byron ratted on me. Wait till I get my hands on him."

"For the past week the good folks in Morgan's Point have been expressing similar sentiments about you."

"Why?"

"Everyone's been speculating about why you felt the need to keep your mission a secret, and it seems they've all jumped to the same conclusion. Even Rachel is mad at you for jilting her sister."

"Hey, I haven't jilted anybody!"

"That's not the word around town." Joe's voice was filled with amusement.

Clay frowned at the receiver. "Well, I hope you set them straight. You did defend me, didn't you?"

"Nope. I gave you my word I wouldn't tell anyone anything, not even my wife. And Rachel is going to have my hide when she finds out I kept this from her."

"They'll all get over it when Molly and I get together."

"So, how's your little scheme coming along?"

"I'm on my way home even as we speak. I should be there sometime after four. Most of the patients should be gone from the clinic by then, as well as that gulag guard of a nurse of hers.''

''You'd better watch your back,'' Joe said emphatically. ''Rachel's really upset. If we were back in my ancestors' days, she'd strap on a six-shooter and call you out. All this anxiety can't be good for a pregnant woman.''

''It hasn't done a lot for me, either,'' Clay complained.

Joe chuckled.

''It's not funny,'' Clay retorted. ''I didn't laugh when you came whining for advice about how to handle Rachel, did I?''

''You didn't laugh. You might have chuckled a little. Is there anything else I can do for you?''

''Yes, keep your angry wife occupied and away from the clinic until I have a chance to talk to Molly.''

''I think I can manage that,'' Joe replied smugly.

It was after four when the truck driver pulled his rig up in front of the clinic and stopped, the brakes making a noisy protest. Clay opened the door and jumped down from the cab.

''Wait right here and don't move,'' he instructed the driver as he slammed the door.

The man frowned and yelled back, ''This rig is blocking the street. Might be violating a weight ordinance or somethin'. Traffic's gonna get jammed up.''

''Don't worry about it. There's not much traffic in Morgan's Point,'' Clay called back. ''Don't move.''

''You're the boss.'' The driver shrugged, turned off the engine and settled back for a catnap.

Clay was relieved that Molly's new nurse was nowhere in sight when he walked up to the reception desk. Heather was on duty, and when she heard him coming, she crammed the book she'd been reading into a drawer. Then she saw who it was, and her nose tilted up. "What do you want?"

"Good afternoon to you, too, Heather. I would very much like to see Molly, if you could trouble yourself to summon her."

The girl examined her fingernails, and her voice was cool. "Dr. Fox, like, doesn't want to see you."

"Come on, Heather, give me a break." Clay was tired of playing games. "I love her."

"Yeah, right. That's why you jilted her."

"I wish people would quit saying that. I didn't jilt her, Heather." Clay didn't know why he felt compelled to explain anything to the girl. "I merely went to St. Augustine on business."

"Monkey business, if you ask me." She picked up a pencil and doodled on a message pad.

"No one asked you, Heather."

"Everybody, like, knows you went there to buy that boat you're always talking about. Just so you can sail off into the sunset and leave Doc."

"I'm not going anywhere." Clay was losing what little patience he had left. "Except maybe on a honeymoon."

Her head jerked around so fast her blond hair flipped itself out of her eyes. "What?"

"I don't have time to explain the concept, Heather," he said from between gritted teeth. "Not that you're old enough to understand."

"Chill out." Heather was apparently relieved to learn his intentions were honorable. "I get it. I read a lot, you know? Doc's in her office going over charts. You want I should tell her you're here?"

"I'm going into the examining room and I want you to tell her she has a patient waiting. Then I want you to skedaddle. Take off early. Lock up and put the Closed sign in the door. Will you do that?" he asked.

Heather nodded and started off down the hall. She stopped suddenly and looked at the floor. "Mr. Cusak, I didn't really think you were a jerk."

"Thank you, Heather. Now I can die a happy man. Oh, and Heather?"

"What?" she whispered.

"Don't tell her it's me."

She rolled her eyes toward the ceiling. "Like, I don't know how to keep a secret or nothin'."

Molly sat at her desk trying to write progress notes, but she had long since lost her concentration. She couldn't stop thinking about Clay. She'd been so sure she was doing the right thing by giving him her endorsement to leave. But now she was beginning to suspect she'd made the biggest mistake of her life. How long would it take to get over him?

Heather knocked once and opened the door. She stuck her head inside. "You've got one last patient, Doc. He's in exam room one."

"Who is it?" Molly asked.

Heather lifted her shoulders. "I gotta go, Doc. See ya."

Molly fluffed her hair, hoping she didn't look as wilted as she felt. There was a sick man waiting for her, and she would just have to put her personal problems on hold. When she didn't find a chart in the bin outside the examination room, she opened the door and then paused on the threshold.

No sick man had ever looked so good.

"Clay?" Molly's hand was frozen on the doorknob. She was happy to see him, but carefully masked her expression. "I'd like to chat about your trip, but I have a patient waiting." Her words were measured and professional. But her heart pounded when she recognized the I-mean-business look on Clay's face.

"That would be me," he said. Then his eyes softened and his whispered words were raw. "Damn, I've missed you, Molly. You look great."

"So do you," she said. She'd known she would have to face him someday. She just hadn't thought it would be so soon. Or so difficult.

"Was I gone long enough?" he asked, sitting down on the end of the paper-covered examining table.

Too long, she thought. "What are you doing here?"

"You're a doctor and you're morally obligated to rid me of pain. Right?"

"Something like that."

"So, come in here and take care of me."

Molly stepped into the room again, but she didn't close the door.

"I'm in a pretty bad way, Doc."

"You don't look sick to me."

"How can you tell that from way over there?" he said logically. "Don't you have to perform a physical examination to determine the status of my health?"

Molly scrutinized him. "What's going on, Clay?"

"Something is seriously wrong with me," he said evasively.

He seemed determined that she play along. "All right. What are your symptoms?"

He thought it over and decided to stick with real ones. "I've suffered an almost total loss of appetite lately."

Molly crossed her arms on her chest. She'd experienced the same thing. "It's probably stress."

Clay could see he was going to have to do better than that. "I can't sleep."

"A common complaint. Again, stress or anticipation of your move might be responsible." She was still waiting to hear a symptom worthy of her time.

He was getting no sympathy. "I have a strange achy feeling here." He pointed to his chest in the general area of his heart.

Molly frowned and stepped toward him as she put the stethoscope in her ears. "Undo the top three buttons of your shirt, please."

Clay's eyes never left hers as he took his time following her instructions. Now they were getting somewhere.

Molly's training and experience allowed her to conceal her nervousness. "How severe is the pain?"

Clay tried to look pitiful. "Extremely severe."

She placed the cold metal against the tan skin on his chest and he flinched. "Where do you keep that thing? In the freezer?"

She smiled and moved it over his clavicle and down to another tender spot, just below his nipple. She enjoyed watching the goose bumps rise. She listened to the strong and steady thump of his heart and then removed the stethoscope from her ears.

"I think I'll call Officer Hacker and ask him to cite you for malingering."

"Is there a law against wanting to get a certain doctor's attention?"

"We'll find out, won't we?"

"What gave me away?"

"There is nothing wrong with you. If you like I could schedule an X ray tomorrow to be sure."

"Listen again, Doc," he entreated. "You must have missed the palpitations I get whenever you're near." He took her hand and pulled her close to him. "It's going crazy now. You're the only one who can cure me."

"Clay," she protested. Molly was amused by his antics, but it was time to stop playing games.

"Listen," he commanded.

Against her better judgment, Molly listened to the jackhammer rhythm. "Clay, what is the point of all this?"

"The point is, Doc, I already know I have an advanced case of bacheloritis."

"What?"

"You heard me. The only known cure for my condition is marriage. That's where you come in. I'm not willing to marry anyone but you. So, do you love me enough to put me out of this misery?"

Molly was having her own cardiac problems. "If I said yes, you'd probably have a real heart attack."

"Try me," he said with a grin. "If I collapse, you can perform mouth-to-mouth resuscitation."

Molly wrenched away from him and stepped back before she could do something rash—such as take him up on the offer before he changed his mind. "You don't want to be married. You need your freedom."

Clay was getting tired of this. "Who the hell made you the authority on what *I* want or need." He raised his voice. "I—" he thumped his chest "—that's me, Clay Cusak. I want to marry you, Molly! I need you!"

"If you wanted to get married so badly, you adventure-seeking fool," she yelled back at him, "why did you go off to St. Augustine to buy yourself a damned boat?"

"I bought it for us," he argued.

"So you can have your cake and eat it, too?" she asked sarcastically. "Now I understand what you have in mind."

"What's that supposed to mean?"

"If you think I'd marry you and let you traipse around the world to God knows where, then let you come home to me whenever the urge strikes, you're dead wrong."

"That's the most absurd thing I've ever heard."

"What's so absurd about it?" She'd been thinking about making the offer herself.

He took her hands in his. "Hey, if I came home every time the urge struck, I wouldn't even make it as far as Lake Sampson."

She didn't know what to say. She did, however, know what to do. She pulled him close for a lingering kiss.

"Oh, Molly, I love you so much."

"I love you, too, Clay."

"I want to marry you." He was encouraged by her eager response. Maybe he could salvage things yet.

"I want to marry you, too. Maybe we could make it work. We'll have each other and you can still have the adventure you crave."

He couldn't believe that she still didn't get it. "Molly, loving you is all the adventure I want in my life. I'm not making any sacrifices by staying in Morgan's Point. That plan I made for sailing off all alone was devised out of loneliness. The night we danced in the high school gym, I realized I've always loved you.

"Ever since then I've thought of little else but you. You've given my life new meaning, and all my dreams are different now."

"Are you sure?" she asked. "Be very, very sure."

"I'm positive."

Molly saw the sincerity in his eyes. This man would never lie to her. "You'd better be. Otherwise the children and I will just come after you every time you try to take off."

Clay grinned. "Molly, my love, if you and our kids don't go, I ain't going!"

His lips had almost found hers again when an air horn blasted from the street. Long and loud. Clay kissed the tip of her nose, instead. "Come outside. I have a surprise for you."

They were on their way out when they heard Officer Hacker's siren. Molly stopped in her tracks at the sight of Clay's surprise. Right in the middle of the street, blocking traffic in all directions, was a truck towing a very large fishing boat. Printed on its hull in oversize letters was the name: *Bachelor Cure*.

Officer Hacker turned off his siren and tried to persuade people who had stopped to gawk to get back in their cars and drive away. No one moved on. They shared Earl Potts's sentiments. "Forget it, Wayne. It ain't every day you see a big boat in the middle of the street."

"Somebody's in big trouble. There are laws against obstructing traffic," Officer Hacker grumbled as he tried in vain to disperse the good citizens who were now coming out of shops and stores to see what all the commotion was about.

"What is this?" Molly asked Clay.

"It's a boat."

"I can see that. What's it doing here?"

"It's on its way to its permanent home on Lake Sampson. I wanted you to see it. There's a great little cabin, perfect for a honeymoon, weekends for two, or three, or four, or more. When the family expands."

He climbed up the rope ladder on the side of the boat. "Come up here and I'll show you around."

Molly put her hand into his and climbed aboard. As he pulled her into his arms, the townspeople cheered.

Officer Hacker sauntered over to the ladder. "This here boat belong to you, Cusak?"

He grinned down at the lawman. "To me and the future Mrs. Cusak," he corrected.

Clad in a plastic cape from Dottie's Kurl Up and Dye salon and dabbing shampoo streaks from her face, Lydia rushed out onto the street in time to hear Clay's announcement.

"That's wonderful news, children," she called to them. "I always knew Clay would be my son someday." She dabbed at tears now.

"Thanks, Mom." Molly looked around at her neighbors and acknowledged their thumbs-up signs and calls of good wishes. She'd never thought her engagement would be such a public event.

"Yeah," Clay seconded. "Thanks, Mom."

Rachel ran up the street. "Is it true?"

"Is what true?" Molly called down.

"Are you and Clay really getting married?"

Molly and Clay exchanged amused glances. "How did you hear about it so fast? I just found out a minute ago," Molly said.

"Well, Dottie called Hattie Benson, and Lillie was in the drugstore and she called Joe, but he was too tired from keeping me busy so I—"

"Never mind, Rachel," Molly and Clay said together. "We know."

"Hey, buddy," the truck driver said, sticking his head out the window, "can we leave now? I got a schedule."

"Sure, let's go," Clay said.

The driver started the engine and, with a great grinding of gears, slowly pulled out. Officer Hacker seemed to remember his duty and jogged alongside.

"Clay, you'd better come on down from there. I need to talk to you. I know you must've violated any number of ordinances, but I may have to go back to the office and look 'em up. This could take a while."

"Sorry, Officer. I'm kind of busy. Can't it wait?" Clay kissed Molly and ignored the long arm of the law.

The truck shifted out of dual low gear, and the policeman, who was scribbling madly on his citation pad, had to double his pace just to keep up. "You can't just go running off, Clay. You broke the law."

Clay showed a wanton disregard for law and order and gave Hacker a get-lost wave.

The officer was running now and his breathing was labored. "Who's gonna sign these tickets?"

Molly and Clay laughed. Their happiness was too complete to be dampened by the mere threat of incarceration.

"I'll stop by and pay them first thing in the morning," Clay called as they picked up speed. They left the poor man in the middle of the street clutching his sides.

For safety's sake, he and Molly sat down on the deck.

"Now that we're finally alone, would you care to explain all this?" she asked.

"I knew it would take a powerful message to convince you I wasn't making a sacrifice, but gaining new life." He looked around at the boat. "Was it powerful enough?"

"It was a grand gesture and I love it." By buying a fishing boat, instead of a yacht, Clay had convinced her that he was content to stay close to home.

"I can't believe you wanted to send me away," he said with a pout.

"I didn't want to. I just wanted you to be happy. That's what I get for believing the old saying about how if you love something you should set it free."

"I am free. Free to choose how I want to spend the rest of my life. I choose you, Molly Fox. Will you marry me?"

"Yes, I will," she said happily, knowing their future would be brighter because the man she had chosen would always make her laugh. She looked around as the countryside sped by. "What are we going to do at Lake Sampson tonight?"

"Skinny-dipping comes to mind," he said with a grin.

She pushed him playfully. "We need to save something for the honeymoon."

He only half pretended disappointment. "I guess we could always go fishing."

"Okay, but there's something you need to know about me that might make you change your mind."

"Nothing could make me do that."

"I don't clean fish," she said with a contented smile.

* * * * *

HE'S MORE THAN A MAN, HE'S ONE OF OUR

Fabulous Fathers

MIRACLE DAD
by Toni Collins

Single father Derek Wolfe didn't think a miracle was too much to ask for when it came to his children's happiness. But when he demanded to leave heaven and return to them, he never considered the consequences. His children didn't recognize him, and their guardian, Evelyn Sloan, thought Derek was her fiancé! Derek found himself in an earthly dilemma—he could step in as father to his children again *only* if he married Evelyn....

Available in May from Silhouette Romance

Fall in love with our FABULOUS FATHERS!

Silhouette
R O M A N C E™

MILLION DOLLAR SWEEPSTAKES (III)
AND
EXTRA BONUS PRIZE DRAWING

SWP-S494

It's our 1000th
Silhouette Romance™,
and we're celebrating!

And to say "THANK YOU" to our wonderful readers, we would like to send you a

FREE AUSTRIAN CRYSTAL BRACELET

This special bracelet truly captures the spirit of CELEBRATION 1000! and is a stunning complement to any outfit! And it can be yours FREE just for enjoying SILHOUETTE ROMANCE™.

FREE GIFT OFFER

To receive your free gift, complete the certificate according to directions. Be certain to enclose the required number of proofs-of-purchase. Requests must be received no later than August 31, 1994. Please allow 6 to 8 weeks for receipt of order. Offer good while quantities of gifts last. Offer good in U.S. and Canada only.

And that's not all! Readers can also enter our...

CELEBRATION 1000! SWEEPSTAKES

In honor of our 1000th SILHOUETTE ROMANCE™, we'd like to award $1000 to a lucky reader!

As an added value every time you send in a completed offer certificate with the correct amount of proofs-of-purchase, your name will automatically be entered in our CELEBRATION 1000! Sweepstakes. The sweepstakes features a grand prize of $1000. PLUS, 1000 runner-up prizes of a FREE SILHOUETTE ROMANCE™, autographed by one of CELEBRATION 1000!'s special featured authors will be awarded. These volumes are sure to be cherished for years to come, a true commemorative keepsake.

DON'T MISS YOUR OPPORTUNITY TO WIN! ENTER NOW!

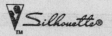

CELOFFER

Don't miss these other titles by favorite author

PEPPER ADAMS!

Silhouette Romance®

#08724	CIMARRON KNIGHT*	$2.25	☐
#08753	CIMARRON REBEL*	$2.25	☐
#08842	THAT OLD BLACK MAGIC	$2.59	☐
#08862	ROOKIE DAD	$2.69	☐
#08897	WAKE UP LITTLE SUSIE	$2.69	☐
#08964	MAD ABOUT MAGGIE	$2.75	☐
#08983	LADY WILLPOWER	$2.75	☐

*Cimarron Stories

TOTAL AMOUNT	$
POSTAGE & HANDLING	$
($1.00 for one book, 50¢ for each additional!)	
APPLICABLE TAXES**	$_____
TOTAL PAYABLE	$_____
(check or money order—please do not send cash)	

To order, complete this form and send it, along with a check or money order for the total above, payable to Silhouette Books, to: **In the U.S.:** 3010 Walden Avenue, P.O. Box 9077, Buffalo, NY 14269-9077; **In Canada:** P.O. Box 636, Fort Erie, Ontario, L2A 5X3.

Name: _____

Address: _____ City: _____

State/Prov.: _____ Zip/Postal Code: _____

**New York residents remit applicable sales taxes.
Canadian residents remit applicable GST and provincial taxes.

PABACK3

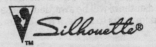

IT'S OUR 1000TH SILHOUETTE ROMANCE, AND WE'RE CELEBRATING!

JOIN US FOR A SPECIAL COLLECTION OF LOVE STORIES BY AUTHORS YOU'VE LOVED FOR YEARS, AND NEW FAVORITES YOU'VE JUST DISCOVERED. JOIN THE CELEBRATION...

April
REGAN'S PRIDE by **Diana Palmer**
MARRY ME AGAIN by **Suzanne Carey**

May
THE BEST IS YET TO BE by **Tracy Sinclair**
CAUTION: BABY AHEAD by **Marie Ferrarella**

June
THE BACHELOR PRINCE by **Debbie Macomber**
A ROGUE'S HEART by **Laurie Paige**

July
IMPROMPTU BRIDE by **Annette Broadrick**
THE FORGOTTEN HUSBAND by **Elizabeth August**

SILHOUETTE ROMANCE...VIBRANT, FUN AND EMOTIONALLY RICH! TAKE ANOTHER LOOK AT US! AND AS PART OF THE CELEBRATION, READERS CAN RECEIVE A FREE GIFT!

YOU'LL FALL IN LOVE ALL OVER AGAIN WITH SILHOUETTE ROMANCE!

CEL1000

CELEBRATION 1000! Free Gift Offer

ORDER INFORMATION:

To receive your free AUSTRIAN CRYSTAL BRACELET, send three original proof-of-purchase coupons from any SILHOUETTE ROMANCE™ title published in April through July 1994 with the Free Gift Certificate completed, plus $1.75 for postage and handling (check or money order—please do not send cash) payable to Silhouette Books CELEBRATION 1000! Offer. Hurry! Quantities are limited.

FREE GIFT CERTIFICATE   096 KBM

Name:_____

Address:_____

City:_____ State/Prov.:_____ Zip/Postal:_____

Mail this certificate, three proofs-of-purchase and check or money order to CELEBRATION 1000! Offer, Silhouette Books, 3010 Walden Avenue, P.O. Box 9057, Buffalo, NY 14269-9057 or P.O. Box 622, Fort Erie, Ontario L2A 5X3. Please allow 4-6 weeks for delivery. Offer expires August 31, 1994.

PLUS

Every time you submit a completed certificate with the correct number of proofs-of-purchase, you are automatically entered in our CELEBRATION 1000! SWEEPSTAKES to win the GRAND PRIZE of $1000 CASH! PLUS, 1000 runner-up prizes of a FREE Silhouette Romance™, autographed by one of CELEBRATION 1000!'s special featured authors, will be awarded. No purchase or obligation necessary to enter. See below for alternate means of entry and how to complete sweepstakes rules.

CELEBRATION 1000! SWEEPSTAKES
NO PURCHASE OR OBLIGATION NECESSARY TO ENTER

You may enter the sweepstakes without taking advantage of the CELEBRATION 1000! FREE GIFT OFFER by hand-printing on a 3" x 5" card (mechanical reproductions are not acceptable) your name and address and mailing it to: CELEBRATION 1000! Sweepstakes, P.O. Box 9057, Buffalo, NY 14269-9057 or P.O. Box 622, Fort Erie, Ontario L2A 5X3. Limit: one entry per envelope. Entries must be sent via First Class mail and be received no later than August 31, 1994. No liability is assumed for lost, late or misdirected mail.

Sweepstakes is open to residents of the U.S. (except Puerto Rico) and Canada, 18 years of age or older. All federal, state, provincial, municipal and local laws apply. Offer void wherever prohibited by law. Odds of winning dependent on the number of entries received. For complete rules, send a self-addressed, stamped envelope to: CELEBRATION 1000! Rules, P.O. Box 4200, Blair, NE 68009.

 ONE PROOF OF PURCHASE

096KBM

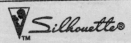